BONNIE ENGSTROM

Natalie's Red Dress

The Candy Cane Girls, book 9

By Bonnie Engstrom

Copyright © 2021 Bonnie Engstrom

Forget Me Not Romances, a division of Winged Publications.

All rights reserved as permitted under the U.S. Copyright Act of 1976. No part of the publication may be reproduced, distributed or transmitted in any form or by any means, or stored in a database or retrieval system, without prior permission of the publisher.

All verses from NLT version

This book is a work of fiction. Names, characters, places, and incidents are the product of the author's imagination and are used fictitiously. Any resemblance to actual events, locales, or persons, living or dead, is coincidental, except for the instances where they were used in conjunction with a business on purpose.

ISBN: 979-8-3302-5714-0

Author's note:

When I started this story it was an inspiration from a dear friend. I had hoped I would be writing it in National Breast Cancer Awareness Month. Unfortunately, I did not finish it in time. Still it is relevant. Please pray as I do for a cure and for better diagnoses and treatments.

Dedication

This book is dedicated to my mother in law, Roberta, and to my dear friend and prayer partner Donna Coosey who described and led me on her personal journey and gave me permission to use it in a story. Thank you, Donna, for sharing. Your honesty and willingness have made all the difference. This book is dedicated to you and the following dear friends, some of whom went through trials like you, and some who are looking down and applauding.

Anita, Judy, Dorothy.

Donna shared some of her personal pain and gave me permission to share it here. Perhaps as you read this story you will understand Natalie's fear, and hopefully it will encourage you and your mothers and sisters and daughters and friends to take advantage of our wonderful technology and get an annual mammogram.

From Donna's emails with her permission:

"I can't stress how important it is to have an annual mammo.

My mammogram showed up with a huge mass. After taking a closer look at it the radiologist suggested that I go see a cancer specialist. I was so scared of what was going to happen. She said the x-rays showed the cells were coming together which is a sign of forming cancer so she sent me back to have a little platelet put in which marks the place. I went back for another mammogram to make sure that they could see it. After that I was taken to a women's center and they put in a marker which shows exactly where they needed to extract the mass. From there it was surgery. It was a very smooth surgery and probably about 15 to 20 stitches and the pain wasn't really bad - the thing that bothered me the most was the little gap that it left on my breast like a little hole. Lumpectomy is what it is called. Surgery took about 45 minutes.

Dr said if this had been left it would grow large if I had not been doing annual test.

Please it is important to have a mammo done once a year. It is not invasive and takes just a few minutes and may save your life. Sometimes you don't even feel what is going on in your breast. Had I not done the mammo I would have never known that a mass was growing in my breast and it would have turn into cancer.

God has not given you the spirit of fear but of but if power, love and a sound mind
2 Timothy 1:7. That is what I used when I had my surgery and I got peace."

U.S. Breast Cancer Statistics

The World Health Organization has announced that

female breast has overtaken lung cancer as the most common cancer diagnosis.

- About 1 in 8 U.S. women (about 13%) will develop invasive breast cancer over the course of her lifetime.
- In 2021, an estimated 281,550 new cases of invasive breast cancer are expected to be diagnosed in women in the U.S., along with 49,290 new cases of non-invasive (in situ) breast cancer.
- About 2,650 new cases of invasive breast cancer are expected to be diagnosed in men in 2021. A man's lifetime risk of breast cancer is about 1 in 833.
- About 43,600 women in the U.S. are expected to die in 2021 from breast cancer. Death rates have been steady in women under 50 since 2007, but have continued to drop in women over 50. The overall death rate from breast cancer decreased by 1% per year from 2013 to 2018. These decreases are thought to be the result of treatment advances and earlier detection through screening.
- For women in the U.S., breast cancer death rates are higher than those for any other cancer, besides lung cancer.
- As of January 2021, there are more than 3.8 million women with a history of breast cancer in the U.S. This includes women currently being treated and women who have finished treatment.
- Breast cancer is the most commonly diagnosed cancer among American women. In 2021, it's estimated that about 30% of newly diagnosed cancers in women will be breast cancers.
- A woman's risk of breast cancer nearly doubles if she has a first-degree relative (mother, sister, daughter) who

has been diagnosed with breast cancer.
- About 85% of breast cancers occur in women who have no family history of breast cancer.
- The most significant risk factors for breast cancer are sex (being a woman) and age (growing older).

More

Don't authors always have more to say?

Natalie's Red Dress is the final story in the Candy Cane Girls Series that began with an author friend Darlene Franklin who actually didn't like the idea. Still, she accepted it and I pressed on. This entire series is dedicated to her.

Sadly, Darlene passed away of COVID on January 1, 2021. Fortunately I told her last year that I would dedicate this series to her.

Still More

Much love and thanks to:

Hubby, Dave, of 55 years making dinner so I can write.
Alice Arenz who has prayed me through so many stories, this one included.
Ann Allen, personal WHA (Word Help Ann), who solved so many Word problems for me.
Cynthia Hickey, publisher who waited patiently for this

book to be finished and who designed the beautiful cover.

ABOUT THE CANDY CANES

Six high school freshmen in Newport Beach, California formed a swim team that became legendary. They won the state relay swim championship four years in a row. In addition to their skill and devotion to daily practicing, they prayed together and vowed to be sisters forever. Another thing that set them apart was they chose their own swimsuits making them a team within a larger team. They chose red and white diagonally striped swim suits. Thus, became known as the Candy Canes. They always will be.

Dear Reader ~

I hope you will enjoy this series that tells the stories of women who are what I call super friends ~ friends who committed as teenagers to prayer and loyalty bound by a moniker. The Candy Cane Girls are a unique group of sister friends. I hope their stories will inspire other young women. They are Sisters of Promise, promises they made when young and promises they've kept for generations.

I am hoping to start an inspiration, a situation or a way to encourage young women, especially teen girls, to write their own stories. I have three teenage granddaughters who are bright and talented but as far as I know do not record their thoughts and experiences. I also pray for other teen girls of friends. It troubles me they are not writing about their lives and experiences. Please join me in praying for an upcoming of young women writers.

As you read through this series, and I hope you will, please note how each book tells a story about individual women, how each struggle with a personal situation and overcomes it. Some of the circumstances they encounter are destined by faith and fate; but all require belief and commitment to each other and to the faith of each. I hope you will read every story to see how Cindy deals with her new love's health issues, and Candy takes her fears into action, and Connie . . . well she has a problem that she overcomes with the help of sweet Jake, her 'problems solving' dog. Jake will appear in many following books. He was my running companion for many years – the dearest dog. But Lola and Happy Arthur are shining woofers in their own stories.

But wait until you get to Natalie and Melanie! They hold the keys to lasting friendship. Their stories are almost legendary.

All stories in the series can be read individually, but you will enjoy them more and understand them more if you read them in order.

Noelle, Cindy, Connie, Candy, Natalie, Doreen and especially Melanie will steal your heart.

You will have fun with the different wedding venues. How many weddings have you attended in an historical place, or in a hospital lobby or a gym? Maybe these will be your first and most memorable.

You will do me a great favor if you enjoyed this series and write a quick, honest review on Amazon or Goodreads. Just a few words mean a lot and encourage others to read it.

Thank you. If you would like to be connected to me for comments and conversation please sign up for my newsletter at www.bonnieengstrom.com and learn about my writing history. You can email me at bengstrom@hotmail.com. Please put SERIES <in caps) in the subject line. I would love to chat with you. Special BONUS! The Candy Cane Series is ideal for group discussion, especially for book clubs. I have a special offer for book clubs for all of my books. If you

are interested please email me at bengstrom@hotmail.com with CLUB <all caps) in the subject line.

Blessings,
Bonnie

PROLOGUE

*E*verything in the room was pink. Even the light coming through the filtered window shades glowed pink. The only non-pink thing was the chair.

Natalie unhooked her bra and draped it carefully over the back of the metal chair with the orange cushion. She folded her tee shirt lengthwise, arms tucked in, to lay across it. To hide the bra? Silly. She was modest but not shy. Why had she chosen a pink bra today? Maybe the one on top of the pile in the drawer?

She studied the watercolor painting on the wall of five women walking together, or were they marching? Two more in the painting and it would have represented the Candy Canes. She stifled a laugh and waited for a knock on the door. Why would a medical facility have a signed, original piece of artwork in a room where only women would see it? And only one woman at a time. The knock startled her and she quickly crisscrossed her arms over her bare chest.

Arita reintroduced herself, laughed pleasantly and held out the pink cotton half-gown to Natalie. "You forgot to put this on."

"Nope. Seems silly. We're both women and you're going to see my breasts anyway."

Arita grinned. "I like your attitude," she said and guided Nat to the huge machine. Nat had been there before, but today was different.

"I want you to have a 3D and an ultrasound, too. Just to be sure." Dr. S's words rang in Nat's ears.

"This will hurt a little," Arita said. "I am so sorry, but it's necessary."

Arita adjusted the overhead thing above Nat and gently placed a breast on the Xray plate. Nat shivered. The cold metal made the room seem even colder.

"Now, hold your breath and don't move."

She almost jumped away. But Arita's steady voice kept her still.

ONE

"*I*'m scared, Mel."

"I know you are. The Pink possibility is super scary." She squeezed Natalie's hand.

"But, remember you are young, only a few years over thirty. You have lots of years ahead to be worried."

The women were sharing coffee in Natalie's kitchen. Melanie was Nat's best friend. The last woman to be accepted into the friendship circle, the women who still prayed with each other for over two decades.

Natalie shrugged her shoulders. "Right! You are right. I am young and strong and healthy. No matter that my great grandma had cancer. That was back in the dark ages before biopsies and modern technology. I have nothing to fear, but fear itself, as a certain president said. Who was that?"

"Before your time," Melanie laughed.

~

Every woman needs a special dress.

Natalie had read that somewhere. Probably from an ad in one of the magazines she subscribed to for Nat's

Gym. Maybe she should go shopping. She hated to shop, never knew what to buy other than workout clothes. Clothing was confusing, especially dresses. Nowhere to wear them. Still, shopping might give her a lift after the scary mammogram experience the other day. She needed something positive, something bright and pretty and fun and special, something girly. Maybe a fancy dress would help. Not that she ever had any occasion to wear one.

Maybe she should call Melanie to go with her. She smiled and mentally shook her head. Nope. She needed to be brave, make her own decision. This excursion should be private. She could do it. She parked in the underground lot at South Coast Plaza and stepped on the escalator. When she stepped off, she was in front of a store window filled with dresses. Was that a sign?

"Every woman needs a special dress," the salesgirl said with an enticing smile.

She dangled a shimmery dress high in front of Nat's face and swayed it sideways. Glitter was sprinkled over the bouncy skirt and sparkled in the fluorescent light. Natalie blinked.

"Red? I don't wear red. Besides, I don't wear dresses."

"No, madam? Why not? You are beautiful. Lovely figure, nice legs. You should wear."

"Uh . . . I'm not a femmy girl." The woman's puzzled expression bothered Natalie.

"I own and run a gym. I guess you could say I'm sort of a jock, a tomboy. I don't wear dresses."

The older woman, why had she called her a sales*girl*?, pulled a tissue from between what her friend Vivian called *the girls* and patted an eye. "So sad. You need to embrace. You have lovely bosoms," she giggled.

"This dress, it will show off the, how you say it, cleavage. Very enticing to suitors." The woman, whose nametag said Venus, smiled warmly and dangled the dress again.

"Embrace?"

"Your womanness. Your . . . fem in in it ee." She dangled the dress again. The delicate fabric brushed Nat's nose. "See. So beautiful. A special dress for a beautiful lady."

Nat laid her credit card on the counter. She preferred to pay cash, but knew if she decided to return the fancy dress, and probably would, it would be easier this way. The woman made a big fuss wrapping the dress in excessive tissue and laying it delicately in a large black box with gold lettering. Before she closed the lid, she folded the tissue over and made an elaborate display of sealing it with a scalloped gold sticker. The box clicked shut and she presented it to Natalie like a gift.

"Such a lovely decision, Madam. This dress will turn heads. Enjoy."

Nat rushed out of the store clutching the box under one arm and dangling her oversized purse from the other. Where was the down elevator? Must be a trick to put it so far away that customers had to continue shopping and not leave. She finally found it and almost tripped trying to get on. She wanted to get out before anyone saw her. Nat, the tomboy, gym woman, didn't shop for fancy clothes. She bought all her workout clothes online, delivered in cardboard boxes the next day. *Steady, Nat. It's just a dress. Your private secret. Then she heard her name.*

"Nattie! Yoo hoo!" Noelle's teacher voice was unmistakable. *What was she doing here? Spying on me?*

Noelle had to have seen the black box. It was almost slipping from under Natalie's arm. After the "Hi," and "Hi," and hugs, Natalie excused herself.

"Sorry, Noelle, gotta run. Need to prepare for my Zumba class tomorrow."

Noelle caught the box just as it slipped lower. "Wow, Natalie, you must have bought a treasure. That store," she said eyeing the gold printing, "has phenomenal clothes. I hope you got a bargain." She giggled and pushed the box back up under Natalie's arm. "Need help? You really need to get a smaller purse."

Nat glanced at Noelle's gold mesh over the shoulder bag. Probably just held her keys and credit card. Not like Nat's that held extra gym shoes and tee shirts and tons of keys to open the gym and lockers and office doors.

"Maybe someday I will. Thanks, No. I can manage."

The women hugged again and Natalie stepped carefully onto the down escalator.

Noelle waved. "See you later."

Nat wondered what that meant. Was she so muddled by her breast cancer worry she forgot about a plan? No, it was just a typical comment. But Noelle never did or said anything typical. She taught Shakespeare to high school students in an advanced class. Everything she did and said had reason. What was she referring to?

TWO

𝒩atalie hung the red dress on a padded lingerie hanger, one she'd inherited from her mother. Or was it Cindy, when she moved to Costa Rica and couldn't take much? So beautiful, so elegant, so not Natalie. She sighed and closed the closet door. Would she ever be brave enough to wear it?

The brr sound startled her and she reached to the vanity counter for her cellphone. Billy. Suddenly her life was filled with men, men she liked, but men she had no feeling toward, other than friendship.

She had prayed so many years for someone special. Someone who had a deep faith like hers. She'd even asked for tall, handsome and rich. Couldn't hurt.

"Hi, Billy. What's up?"

"Just checking about tomorrow. You still want to go to the food thing in Newport Center?"

Every year the Newport Beach community staged a weeklong food tasting extravaganza. All of Fashion Island shopping mall, and part of quaint Corona del Mar, had mini booths along the sidewalks and close to the sponsoring restaurants. Those who signed up for $5 treats even had to stand in line with their tickets. There was always a special event in Newport Beach. The town hosted arts shows and golf fund-raisers, even boat parades that took place on the Bay. This week it was the Tasting Festival to showcase the unique restaurants.

What was wrong with her? She loved to eat, especially unique foods.

"I think I am. Not feeling hungry right now. But I will be ready at six tomorrow. Okay?"

"Hopefully by tomorrow you will have an appetite."

Natalie hung up, pulled off her workout shoes and kicked them aside. Ugh, smelly.

~

"I just can't get into the tasting, Mel. Not in the mood."

"Gosh, Nat, it's food. You love food. And, you can't disappoint Billy."

Melanie heard a loud sigh on the other end of their phone conversation. So not like Natalie who was always upbeat and positive. "Maybe you need a group boost? I bet some of the girls can come over. We could do the pizza thing."

"Yeh, we haven't done that for a long time. Remember last time? When we added so many ingredients it was disgusting?"

"Yep. Who adds mustard and ketchup to pizza?" Mel laughed. "Us, I guess. The notorious Candy Canes."

"My fav was the pineapple. But I guess that's not so unusual."

"Yeh, Hawaiian pizza."

"How about the capers and crushed peanuts? You sort of liked that combo."

"Yeh, both salty. Go together."

"Let's order the basic, plain cheese, and see what you have in your skimpy pantry." Thank goodness Melanie had alerted the other women in a whispered group phone message. Fortunately, Natalie never questioned Mel's pizza party suggestion. Maybe she was too wrapped up in worry.

BONNIE ENGSTROM

THREE

"We need music."

Melanie took off her jacket and tossed it on the back of a barstool at Natalie's kitchen counter.

"I guess. But you know I'm partial to jazz."

"How about Dave Brubeck? We heard him that time when we were exploring."

"Yeh, at that college."

"It was a great concert. Let's play it for inspiration."

Melanie found Brubeck's Take Five on iTunes and told Alexa the invisible girl to play it. Speaking to a small round globe was still foreign to her. Maybe she should get one.

"So, what should we experiment with this time? What weird ingredients?"

"I'm looking to see what you have, Nat. Boy, you don't have much."

"I don't eat much. Not a lot, anyway. Not much variety."

"Yuk! Sauerkraut. Why would you even keep that? Or, why did you buy it?"

"Was on sale. Heard it was healthy. Don't give me that look."

Melanie grinned and pulled out a can. "Here's something that might be fun, and crunchy."

"Water chestnuts? Strange on pizza, but okay."

Melanie set an array of containers on the counter. Cans, bottles and bags. She started opening and dumping into bowls, and some she threw away.

"Why are you tossing the tuna? That might be fun on pizza."

"Because," Mel sighed, "the date says two years ago."

"Oh."

"This might work." She opened a can of crab flakes.

"That's saved for my favorite dip."

"Too late."

"Don't toss the capers. I love capers. On anything."

"Oops, phone. You gonna answer that?"

"Maybe." Nat pulled the phone out of her jean pocket. "The caller ID says Hoag Hospital. Why would the hospital be calling me?"

"Why are you clutching your throat, Nat? What's wrong?"

"Could be the doctor. He called me from the hospital number once before. I'm scared, Mel. Why is he calling me now?"

Melanie wrapped her arms around her friend. Holding her close she said, "I think you'd better answer."

"I'll take it in the bedroom. For privacy."

Melanie had no chance to worry when she heard the door open with loud female laughter. Noelle and Candy pushed inside giggling and elbowing each other.

"Me first." Noelle's blue eyes glittered with

amusement. She pushed aside her blonde bangs, put her hands on her hips and said in teacher-like authority. "I brought the jicama. Can't have pizza without it."

"Yes we can," Candy argued. Flipping auburn curls over her shoulder she banged a plastic container shaped like a bear on the counter. "I brought the honey. Super yummy."

Melanie knew the women were teasing each other. Their banter was part of their firm friendship. Not having grown up with them she was still getting used to it. She swallowed hard and bit her lip remembering how grateful she was to be part of the group. She began to arrange more ingredients on the counter with a can opener.

"Where's Nat?" The two women asked in tandem.

"Bedroom. Taking a phone call." Melanie hesitated. "From the doctor."

"Oh. Bad?"

"Don't know. Yet."

"Hey," Candy said grabbing the others' hands, "Let's pray."

BONNIE ENGSTROM

FOUR

"She's been in there a long time." Candy released the other women's hands from prayer.

"Well," Mel said, "he might be explaining, going into detail. Docs tend to do that, be specific."

"I'm worried," Noelle said. "Too long for a basic conversation."

The front door burst open again. "Yoo-hoo! I'm here," a melodic voice rang out.

Melanie, Candy and Noelle hugged Doreen. "Stop, girls. I love you, but I want to live after tonight." Doreen laughed and tossed her head of dark curls. "I almost couldn't get away from Bill. He wanted to come, too. 'Course you know he's a pizza freak." She glanced at the others.

"What about Vivian? Did you invite her?"

"Oh, my, oh, my," Candy gasped. "We forgot Mom."

~

"It's okay, girls. Please don't knock what little stuffing I have left out of me. You're making my hair grayer." Vivian squirmed away from the group embrace and laughed. "I am honored to be part of this. What is it? A celebration? A wake? No, must be a celebration." She set a jar of pickles on the counter and sniggered. "My contribution. Couldn't think of anything else unique. It's Big Bill's favorite, so use it with reverence. Oops. There's the doorbell. Chiming sound? Did Nat install a new doorbell?"

"It's one of those Ring bells, with a video. Has a special sound," Mel said. "Maybe you and Bill should get one. They are kind of neat, and neighbors can also see what's happening at your home when you aren't there so they can alert you."

"Mmm. Francine and her dog Sam are always there when we go out. I think we are doubly protected," she laughed. "I don't think Big Bill would approve." Laughing again, she said, "Let's get going with the pizza party now that the funny doorbell told us the crust is here." She raced to the door with credit card in hand, then came back with four cardboard boxes.

"Whew! Heavy."

"Sorry, Viv. We should have helped you. Didn't think," Doreen said. "Too distracted worrying about Nat."

"It's okay. Assemble, girls. What are the strange ingredients tonight?"

"Well," Noelle said, "tonight we have capers, canned chili and potatoes and sauerkraut, water chestnuts, crab flakes, honey. And thanks to you, Viv, pickles."

"That's not enough. What else? Nothing way off the wall? Where are the anchovies? Bill loves those, and I promised to take a slice home for him. If I can bear the smell."

"Yeh, he is our Swedish patriarch," Mel laughed. "Gotta appease the big man."

Vivian spread her arms and looked around. "Where is our Natalie? She's the host."

"In the bedroom. With a doctor." Melanie shrugged. "Scared," she whispered.

"She has a doctor in her bedroom?" The girls burst into giddy laughter at Vivian's pizza proportioned eyes.

"No, silly mom, she is on the phone with one. A doctor." Candy hugged her mom, then turned away to dump ingredients on the four pizza crusts.

Vivian tugged her daughter's arm. "What's wrong, Candy? Tell me."

BONNIE ENGSTROM

FIVE

*M*elanie raised her hand to hold Candy off. "Hope you don't mind if I explain. Viv needs to know, and you sometimes get too emotional, Can."

Candy shrugged. "Yes, Mom, Mel can explain better. She knows."

"Let's go into the living room, Vivian." Melanie led the older woman by her hand. She gestured Vivian to the side chair near the brick fireplace. Flames flickered casting early evening shadows on the slate floor. Thank goodness someone had thought to ignite the fake logs. Warmth is important in serious situations.

Still holding Vivian's hand, she pulled the chair closer to the sofa to whisper. "She's scared."

Vivian shook her head and shrugged her shoulders.

"It's fear of pink."

"She doesn't like pink? The color or the retail place?"

Melanie hugged her stomach with mirth. Grasping Viv's hand tighter she said, "Nope. Probably likes both. Do you know what pink for a health diagnosis means,

Viv?"

"Oh. Cancer. Breast cancer."

Vivian wiped her eyes on her sleeve. "We must help her. Now."

~

Natalie closed her bedroom door behind her with a click and smiled widely at the other women. "Hi, there!"

"Well?" The women all turned to Natalie and spoke in babbled unison.

"Why are you so pale?"

"What did the doctor say?"

"Share."

"Stop!" Natalie yelled and spun away, stood rigid, raised her shoulders, then turned back with a grin. "What fun things are we putting on our pizza tonight?" she asked in a restrained voice. "I'm hungry."

Vivian reached to take Nat's hand, but Mel stopped her. "Not yet, Viv. Give her some time."

SIX

Noelle grabbed Melanie's wrist and pulled her outside.

"The patio? Why are we talking on the patio?" Melanie asked. "Oh, got it!"

"Most privacy in this place," Noelle explained. "Very disturbed about her."

"Yes, she isn't handling it well. Natalie our tough girl. It must be scary."

"But she isn't sharing. We can't help if she doesn't."

"How about we do a group thing tomorrow at our fav Starbucks place in Corona del Mar? We can call Cindy and Connie and do a group phone prayer."

"Great idea, Mel. What time? Can you plan it?"

~

Melanie waved to the young woman behind the counter.

"Hi, Sydney! Got a table big enough for a few?"

"Sure. You girls having a confab?" Melanie noticed the barrista's eyes seemed to be following her. The aroma of chocolate and coffee filled her senses. Maybe some cinnamon, too. Nothing better than coffee on a chilly morning, a prayer morning. She laid her cellphone on the table in the far corner. She was ready. Would the others be, too?

"Just a group chat," Mel replied. Had she smiled enough to make the meeting seem casual? Maybe this coffee shop wasn't as private as she thought.

~

Noelle, Doreen and Candy came into Starbucks laughing like naughty five-year olds with hands caught in the cookie jar. Made sense to Melanie since she and Candy were both preschool teachers.

Vivian joined them and shook the mist out of her silver hair. Grinning crookedly, she smiled and asked, "What now?"

"Has anyone checked on Nat this morning?" Noelle inquired.

"I tried to call. No answer," Candy said.

"I did, too. No answer," Doreen echoed.

"Now I'm worried." Mel's forehead wrinkled. "Let's go over there. Now!"

~

Four cars and Candy's motorcycle parked in front of Nat's condo. Neighbors peeked out of windows, and one woman in curlers wearing a pink flowered robe stood on her porch hugging her chest. "What's going on?" she shrieked.

"Just checking on a friend."

"I hope so. The girl has a weird schedule, up and out early and home late."

"She owns a gym, so has to be there for her clients. You don't know?"

"Uh, no. Never have time to ask. Too busy. She a

good girl?"

"Super good," Mel laughed. "Very nice girl," she added wondering what made the woman so busy.

"Glad to hear it. Maybe I can bring her some of my cookies." The plastic curlers bobbled.

Mel suppressed a chuckle. "I'm sure she would love them. How nice."

"Does she eat stuff like that? Being a gym girl?"

"She loves food, so, yes. Thanks so much for being a good neighbor."

Curler lady gave a thumbs up, turned around and edged up to her open door.

"Who's out there, Gladys?"

"Never mind, Earl. Just a neighbor. Go back to the TV."

Noelle grabbed Melanie's arm. "Enough of this nonsense. Come on."

"Okay. I know where the not so secret key is."

"Maybe we should ring or knock first? Not just burst in?" Vivian suggested. Doreen and Candy nodded.

"Probably," Mel said, "but knowing Nat she won't answer. Still, let's try."

BONNIE ENGSTROM

SEVEN

"What?" Natalie's voice cracked. She opened the door and shoved fingers through tousled blonde hair. "Why are you all here?"

For once Melanie was speechless. She turned to the others with raised brows.

"Just checking on you, Nat." Candy's voice lilted. "Wanna come to Starbucks for a cup of coffee?"

"Not dressed. Thanks." Natalie shoved at her hair again and rubbed a knuckle across an eye. "But I do have that fancy coffee maker and lots of pods for it. Wanna come in?" Her invitation sounded reluctant but it had been said.

The women crowded around the small kitchen table and bumped elbows. Candy grinned at Noelle, Noelle winked at Doreen, Melanie snickered. Vivian hem-hawed.

Natalie had run to the bedroom and thrown on some purple sweats. Five minutes later she pulled up a barstool and loomed over the others.

"So tell. Why? Worried about me?" Blank faces

stared back. "Don't."

"Don't what?" Noelle asked. "Don't worry? Don't care?"

Vivian's chair scraped the tile when she stood up. She put her arms around Natalie and hugged tight. "We care, Nat. We really do. We know you are going through . . . something." She paused, and the other women nodded. "Please share. Please. We are all here for you. You know that. I hope."

"I can't explain."

"Why?" Melanie asked. "Scared?"

Natalie nodded and ran to the bathroom. The door slammed kerplunk. Then running water.

"What do you think she's doing?" Doreen asked.

"I don't think she's flossing her teeth." Vivian said glaring at the others. "You don't hear the sobbing?"

~

"Let's clean up." Doreen started rinsing and tossing. "Then go, and leave her alone."

"NO!" Candy and Noelle stopped drying and dropped their dish towels. Mel shook her head and crossed her hands over her chest. "We can't. We have to know how to help her. Not abandon her. Don't you understand?"

"I do," Vivian said. "Maybe it's my age, or memories, but I really do."

The girls looked at Vivian, but Candy answered.

"Mom had a scare some years ago, when I was a kid. But I remember hearing her sobbing behind the bathroom door and running the water to try to muffle it. Scared the you know what out of me."

"Yes," Vivian nodded. "But I got through it. Almost destroyed my marriage to Candy's dad." She sighed and started to pace around the room. "At least," she gulped, "at least Natalie doesn't have that to burden her with."

Seeing the girls' expressions, she lowered her head and covered her eyes. "What a horrible thing to say. I am so ashamed."

"It's okay, Mom." Candy grabbed Vivian's hand. "It was a hard time for you. You didn't mean it the way it sounded. We know that."

"Oh, but I did, in a way. At least Nat doesn't have a husband to disappoint, to stare at a mangled breast. Or a missing one. That was the worst fear of all."

~

"What do we do now?" Noelle slid open the glass door and stepped out into the damp air.

The women huddled on the patio again. The morning was still chilly. June gloom in Newport Beach seemed to hang on forever. An errant breeze drifted from the Pacific two miles away. Salty. Doreen shivered and pulled her sweater around her shoulders.

"We have to do something," she said. "We have to help her." She wiped a tear with a crumbled tissue and turned toward Noelle. "You were all there for me during the worst two traumas of my life during my accident and when that woman accused Bill of fathering her child. We must be here for Natalie."

Melanie covered her face and choked.

"What's wrong, Mel?"

Doreen wrapped arms around her and held tight. "It's okay, Mel. It really is. God worked it all out. I was, am, blessed."

"But it was me. I was the one who caused your accident. Because of me you have one shorter leg."

"Shh." Doreen put a finger to Melanie's lips. "In the

past. I forgave. You accepted, sweet friend. The accident gave me a fabulous career and a devoted husband." She hugged Melanie again. "Time to help Natalie."

Candy looked at Melanie and gripped her hands. "You. You, Mel, are the best one to help."

"Why me?" Melanie asked wiping tears. "We can all help."

"Yes, but you are closest to Nat. From what you told us you know more details. You can share with the rest of us, and we can pray. But you need to be her advocate. You."

EIGHT

Melanie parked in the slot closest to the church office and pushed open the door wondering why it opened in instead of out.

"Can I help you? Oh, it's you Melanie," receptionist Kathleen looked up. "Do you have an appointment with a pastor?" She looked down at the schedule in front of her.

"No. Sorry. I know Pastor Lyn is usually here on Tuesday, so I was hoping to visit with her briefly."

"She usually is, but today she is scheduled to be at the Huntington Beach campus."

"Who's asking for me?" Lyn swung open an adjacent door. "Melanie? That you?"

"Me, Pastor. Do you have a few minutes?"

"For you, dear, absolutely. Kathleen, please cancel my Huntington Beach situation." Squinting her eyes she peered over the counter to see the schedule. "I wasn't due there for a few hours. Anyone there make an appointment?"

"No" Kathleen looked up. "So I guess you're free to

stay here."

Melanie sat near the end of the sofa in Lyn's small office and crossed her ankles.

"You seem very uncomfortable, dear. Relax and tell me what's troubling you. I know you only come to see me when you have questions." Lyn brushed her blondish gray hair aside and pushed it behind her ears.

"It's about a friend." The words were barely a whisper.

She felt the warmth of Lyn's hands covering hers and leaned into her shoulder. A strong shoulder. As always, the older woman prayed for guidance. After learning about Natalie, she spoke.

"Scary. I won't deny it. She's so young. But God doesn't cater to age, nor does the evil one."

The two women nodded in unison and clasped hands tighter.

"What I want to know," Mel said, "is how to support her, what to say and what to do. The prayer part I know. I and her other friends pray constantly for her. But we feel so alienated. Confused. We want to help with words and things to do. That," she said with tears on her cheeks, "is the question."

~

Mel gripped the steering wheel of her little car, hard. She didn't feel much better. Pastor Lyn was a dear, and Melanie knew she would pray. But, was prayer enough? She turned into Bayview to visit Nat then felt a thunk. Her hands flew off the steering wheel and her forehead slammed into it. What was that tightness? Oh, seatbelt.

A bang on her window roused her. She pressed the button to open it and rubbed her brow with her knuckles.

"Are you all right? I guess we didn't see each other.

Can you step out?" a deep voice asked.

A hand opened her door and pulled her out. Who was this person? He smelled good. Silly thought.

"Who are you? What happened?"

"Alan Spaulding."

A long arm pulled a card from a pocket. "Here's my license. Are you okay?"

"Don't know," Mel answered in a shaky voice. "I guess."

"Should I call 911? Or anyone?"

"Not yet. Please tell me what happened."

"Can't say for sure, but I think we were both going a bit fast and in the same direction. Or maybe from opposite directions," he added. He tipped a square jaw and gave an apologetic grin. Was he embarrassed? Melanie fixated on a lock of blond hair that hung above brown brows and wanted to push it back. Crazy observation. She shook her head and tried to collect her senses. Thinking fast she suggested, "Let's sort it out at my friend's. Over here," she gestured to Nat's condo. "Okay?"

"I will follow you."

~

"It's me, Nat. Mel." Melanie's fist ratta-tat-tatted.

"I don't usually bang on her door, but since you are here . . ."

The tall man grinned. "Totally appropriate. Glad you did."

The door cracked and Natalie peered out squinting. "What? Who's that?"

"Uh, slight problem, Nat. Need to explain. Can we come in? Please?"

Natalie nodded and pulled the door wide to reveal a

messy kitchen and strange smells.

"Why are you in your jammies at this time of day?"

"Why not!" Natalie rubbed her nose. "Why are you criticizing me, Mel? I thought you were my friend."

"You know I am. Sorry to interfere," she smiled. Was that enough of an apology? "But," she continued, "there's been a slight accident we need to sort out, and since it happened here in front of your condo, well . . . I thought maybe at your place would be best. Rather than on the street," she added.

"Accident? You okay?" Natalie turned to the other person with raised brows. "Who is this? Who are you?"

"Alan Spaulding, Ma'am." He produced a card and held it out. His smile was captivating. At least Melanie thought. Maybe Natalie didn't.

"Don't shove it away, Nat. He's trying to be nice."

"But he caused your accident. How nice is that?"

NINE

*M*elanie wrinkled her nose and sniffed.

"Sorry about the smell. Too tired to clean up." Natalie lowered her head and turned shoving her hands in her pajama pockets. "Got to get changed. 'scuse me." A door banged, and Melanie and Alan were alone.

Mel shrugged. "Gonna clean up."

"I'll help. Where's a dish towel?"

"Kind of you," Mel said as she handed him a wrinkled one. They both smiled. His was nice. She started to twist her striped towel into a knot then shook it out and began wiping.

"Pretty ridiculous situation, huh?" Alan laughed holding his angular nose against the smell.

"Don't be too hard on her. She's going through something."

"Why are you crying? Seems like it's hard on you, too." Alan put a gentle hand on Mel's arm.

"Thanks. That's what friends are for. Support." She wiped her eyes on the corner of her towel. "Now, if you really mean to help, let's get to work."

~

Melanie and Alan were quietly wiping dishes when Natalie burst in.

"What are you doing? No, no, no! Stay out of my kitchen."

Natalie grabbed the towels from both of them and tossed them on the sink counter. "My house. I am in charge."

Alan's face blanched then turned crimson. He retreated to an armchair and crossed an ankle over a knee. "Nice reception. You're welcome for the help, lady."

Natalie spread her legs and put her hands on her hips. "Who are you?" she sputtered. "I didn't invite you here."

"No. Your friend did." Alan waved a hand toward Melanie and stared at Natalie with raised brows. "I accepted her gracious invitation."

"Then go, mister. Go."

"Can't. Have something to settle." He paused. "With Melanie. Maybe you, too."

Natalie turned to Melanie. "Mel, explain," she whimpered. "Please."

"It's okay, Nat. Really. He's a nice man. My fault. I invited him to sort something out."

Mel saw Nat's eyes questioning. "We had an accident. Right in front of your condo. Made common sense to come inside instead of standing in the cold."

"Oh." Natalie wiped her palms on her sweat pants. She gestured. "Sit."

~

Melanie stood on the front stoop at Natalie's shaking Alan's hand.

"Sorry about all this. Didn't realize she was so

distraught. I mean upset." She lowered her head and almost whispered, "She's such a sweet person. Usually."

"I'm sure she is. I hope you can help her. I'm glad we sorted out our problem. I'll call my insurance company in the morning."

"I'll call mine, too. Surely there must be other accidents where both parties agree they were equally at fault."

"Or, maybe we will each have to pay for the damage to the other's car," he laughed. "In that case, you would only owe a pittance. Or maybe nothing since mine is a rental and I took out extra insurance." He smiled broadly and squeezed Mel's hand.

"Hey, what were you doing here anyway?" She asked. "Obviously you weren't coming to see Nat," she grinned.

"I guess I never told you. I was coming to surprise my cousin. I haven't seen her since she and Kent were married last year. Thought I'd drop in. Took a wrong turn."

Melanie raised her brows. "Just like that on practically newlyweds?"

"Dumb guy thing, huh?"

"Well, if you were close . . ." Her voice trailed off.

"We grew up together. Our dads were brothers. Our moms were close, too. Best friends." He pulled his hand from Mel's and found something interesting to look at on his shoes. "Guess I miss her. And since I was in the area, thought I'd stop in." He paused to search Mel's face. "Bad idea, huh?"

"Yes. No. A nice idea. But, it's a little late tonight now. Don't you think?"

"Yes. I'll go back to my hotel for the night. I have

another few days of vacation, so might as well take advantage of this beautiful beach town." Alan touched her arm. "Hey, you're shivering."

Melanie nodded. "Newport gets cold at night. Wind from the Pacific. I'm okay, used to it." She smiled tugging on her sleeves and pulling her sweater across her chest.

Alan smiled and tilted his head. "You'd better get home and get warm. Any chance we can see each other again? Except in court?" he teased.

"Sure, Alan," she laughed. "If you really mean that it would be great. Come to Starbucks on the Coast Highway in Corona del Mar in the morning. I'm meeting my friends there at nine. You can meet a lot of them, the Candy Canes, maybe give us some male advice about Nat since you met her tonight."

"Candy Canes? Do you all wear red stripes?"

"They did once, years ago. That's another story. We will explain tomorrow." She hesitated and searched his face. "I should warn you we pray a lot. For each other. It's something we do, have done for almost twenty years. We will probably have a group prayer for Nat. You okay with that?"

"Uh, guess so. I was raised in church, so it doesn't offend me. But I don't pray much anymore." He paused. "You pray for each other in a group?"

Melanie nodded.

"What a concept." Taking a breath, he said, "I will be there for sure. Coffee for all is my treat."

"There's at least five of us. Plus, some spouses." She rolled her eyes. "That's a lot of coffee."

"Well maybe you can get your own refills," he laughed.

TEN

𝓕ortunately, Starbucks wasn't crowded. Only one lone man sat near the front bent over his laptop. Melanie had an aha moment. He looked so much like Jaeda. But she knew Jaed was in Scottsdale with Connie so she smiled and walked by. There was a large round table in the back corner. She preferred outdoors, but with so many coming it would be too crowded on the sidewalk and not as private. She ordered her Venti Carmel Macchiato with an extra splash of caffeine and settled into the half booth. This particular Starbucks in Corona del Mar had become a traditional meeting place for the Candy Canes.

Big Bill had proposed to Vivian here. Connie had enticed Jaeda by rubbing his ankle with her shoe while his little dog Jake looked on. Doreen met Bill here to discuss, oops argue, about the threat to their marriage. The girls loved that Sydney was usually the barista on Saturday mornings. Familiar helped. Melanie chuckled to herself. Sydney most likely knew all their secrets and could probably write a book. Bestseller? Maybe at least in Newport Beach.

"Yoo hoo!" Vivian's greeting bounced off the walls as she blew a kiss. She was so old-fashioned, but being seventy-plus excused her. Big Bill Lord was stomping behind her with a scowl on his face.

"Where's everyone?" he bellowed. "Thought there would be a crowd."

"Coming, Bill. Be patient," Mel whispered when she hugged him.

Noelle burst in with Braydon in tow. Then Candy and Will followed Doreen and Bill, Junior.

"So many Bills!" Melanie laughed. "Can we keep all of you straight?" she quipped as she spied a lone figure hesitating near the door.

"Here's our new friend." Mel waved and walked forward to meet him.

Leading Alan by the hand she introduced him to the crowd. He nodded politely toward a bunch of questioning faces.

"I like his smile," Candy said.

"I like your grin." Vivian said.

"Who are you?" Big Bill asked confrontationally.

"He's my new insurance buddy," Mel said. "We met last night. Actually collided last night. I invited him."

"Because?" Noelle asked.

"You will learn soon. Didn't Shakespeare say something like 'To be or not to be. That is the question'?"

"Touché!" Noelle laughed.

Melanie turned to Alan. "Noelle teaches Shakespeare."

"Oh, got it."

"So, everyone, I want you to meet Alan Spaulding, our new friend."

Everyone said "Hi" and "Welcome." Except Doreen who fiddled with her bracelet. Finally, she spoke.

"Spaulding? Familiar name. Let me think." She pressed a finger to her brow then raised it in an Aha! Gesture. "Had a bride named Spaulding last year. Mmm, Rita?"

Alan's face lit up. "My cousin!"

Doreen nodded. "Very nice lady. Nurse, right?"

"She was one of the nurses at baby Bray's birth," Noelle chimed in.

"I remember her email about a birth where so many people crowded into the waiting area. So funny!" Alan's hands spread melodramatically. "Was that you folks?"

"Probably," Melanie said. "We were all there waiting impatiently for little Braydon's cry."

"How fun to meet you all. Can't wait to tell Rita."

The frivolity finally settled down so Melanie could explain how she and Alan met.

"Serendipity." Someone said.

"A God thing." Another said.

"Destiny," from another.

When Alan went to pay for all the orders and his back was turned, more comments erupted.

"Cute guy, Mel."

"Really nice, Mel. Don't let this one go."

"Yep, a God thing."

Melanie felt heat rising in her face. "Shh, please. It's not like that. We only met last night, under difficult circumstances. Yes," she nodded, "he seems very nice. But our relationship is only friendship. At this point," she added with a wink.

"Why is your face red, Mel?" Vivian asked. "Oops. Sorry. Making an assumption."

Alan came back to the table holding two overloaded trays. Fortunately, each cup had a name scribbled on it. He turned to Melanie.

"I thought we were here to pray for Natalie."

Nine pairs of eyebrows raised.

Big Bill broke the moment of silence. "Let's get on with it."

Vivian squeezed his hand. "Not all of us know why Nat needs prayer," she said calmly. "Melanie, please explain. And explain how our new friend Alan is involved."

Melanie sighed loudly, clasped her hands together and with moist eyes said, "It all started like this."

ELEVEN

After explaining about last night and the kitchen mess and the smell and her attempt and Alan's to clean up, she picked up her phone and began to dial.

"What?" Alan questioned.

"Oh, sorry. Calling Cindy in Costa Rica and Connie in Scottsdale. It's a group thing. We all pray together. Their husbands Rob and Jaeda do, too."

"Wow! I am impressed."

Melanie finally connected to Connie and Jaeda, but Rob said Cindy was ministering to a neighbor, so he was in charge of little Robby. They could hear whimpering in the background.

"Sorry everyone. Potty training. Cindy can call you. Okay?"

Everyone laughed, and exclamations supported Rob. "Good dad."

"Poor Rob stuck with the poopies."

"Such a good guy."

After the comments subsided, the group took hands around the table. Melanie felt Alan's in hers, but she wasn't sure whose hand he clasped with his other one. Almost everyone prayed aloud for Natalie, some with Scriptures, some with whispers, some with choking tears.

Ten minutes later, Big Bill said, "I felt the Holy Spirit. I know I heard Him groan."

Mel's phone chimed. Cindy.

"Hi, gang. Rob told me. I've been praying on my walk back to our place. Fill me in, please.
Rob said he prayed while watching Robby on the potty," she laughed.

~

Alan and Melanie walked out to their cars together. They'd both had to park down the street in the supermarket lot since parking on Pacific Coast Highway was limited and nearly impossible.

"I'll wait until you get in your car and make sure it starts. Did you call your insurance company?"

"I did. They are sending an adjuster to look at my car tomorrow." She reached out her hand to grasp his. "Thanks, Alan, for coming. I hope it wasn't too much for you."

"It was enlightening. And, wonderful. Especially the friendship part with so many of you caring for each other." He peered at Melanie. "Why are you grinning?"

"Just happy I suppose. I always feel happy when we all pray together."

"Even for a sad reason?"

"Even for that."

"Why? Explain please."

"Because I know God is listening. I know He listens closely when we all pray together." She paused to search his face. "Do you know the verse about when two or three pray together?"

"Sort of. Heard it in Sunday school as a kid. I will look it up."

"Thanks for coming, Alan. It was nice having you."

Her little car started fine. She pulled out of the parking space and waved. Alan waved back.

BONNIE ENGSTROM

TWELVE

$\mathcal{A}$lan jerked awake. The pain in his leg was excruciating. He knew it would help if he got up and paced. "Exercise, stretch," the doctor had repeated. Maybe he'd bumped it again getting out of the car the second time to make sure Melanie was all right. He chuckled at the thought of bumping. That's about all their two cars did with each other's the other night. Still, hers had more damage than his, and his was a rental. The muscles in his calf started to relax as he walked around the hotel room.

"So glad I popped for the mini suite now that I'm staying longer than planned," he mumbled. The room didn't answer, and he laughed remembering he read once that people who talked to themselves were extremely intelligent. "Not sure about that, but I'll take it," he said, laughing again. "So, room, what is wrong with Natalie? Pretty girl, but distraught."

He remembered some words in the prayer. Comfort, healing, peace. But he didn't know why. Why were they praying for Natalie? Was it too early to call Melanie?

The bedside clock said 7:30. His phone said 7:32. So much for accuracy. He made a cup of coffee in the in-room coffee carafe, poured in the three mini creamers and stepped out on the narrow patio that came with the mini suite. *So lucky! The Back Bay is beautiful. Maybe I should really stretch the leg and take a run. Wish I had a dog to run with. Mmm. Didn't Melanie say she has a dog? Or was he just hoping?*

Using the dog as an excuse to call her so early, he was cheered by her lilting voice. Surely, he wasn't smitten by a woman he'd only met a day ago. But she was pretty cute with that long wavy hair. And what's with the hat? *Wonder what her story is.*

"You're still here in Newport, Alan. How nice. I was just going to take Lola for a walk. Wanna join?"

Was it karma? No, she probably didn't believe in that with her faith. Coincidence? Or a God thing? He'd sort it out later.

"I was hoping to go for a run on the Back Bay. Would you and Lola join me?" Not usually impromptu he decided to add, "Breakfast at the Marriott after. Good buffet."

"That sounds delightful, Alan. But sweet Lola isn't much of a runner. She's a puller, tugger and a stop often to sniff and pee dog. Jake, Connie and Jaeda's little dog, is the runner dog."

"That's okay. Walking might be better and give us a chance to talk."

They met outside the hotel entrance where Alan was waiting when Melanie pulled up. Lola wiggled and greeted him, then pranced on her hind legs.

"Wow! Someone who's excited to meet me. Maybe you should buy her one of those ballet dancer outfits.

Rita had one when she was a little girl. I think they're called tutus?"

The one block walk to the Back Bay trail was quiet. But when Alan began questioning Melanie about Natalie, Mel clammed up. Finally, she asked, "Did you want to spend time with me? Or do you want answers I can't give?"

"Bad choice on my part, Mel. May I call you Mel?" She only nodded and kept a tight grip on Lola's leash.

"I'm sorry. I really do want to get to know you better. Truly. But your friend's behavior troubled me." He turned to Melanie. "None of my business."

Melanie nodded again and smiled. "Okay. Let's talk about you. What do you do for a living? Why are you here. I know you came to see your cousin, but have you seen her yet?"

"I work in IT, information technology. Have maximum government clearance. Probably shouldn't say that, but I trust you." He paused to take a deep breath. "I'm on sabbatical, so using this time for R and R. And I love it here in Newport. And no, I haven't contacted Rita yet. Not sure why, but I know she has a strange schedule as a nurse." He cleared his throat. "What's that phrase you and your friends say? God's timing?"

"Yes, because He made time, His timing is often different than ours."

He stopped walking and looked her full in the face. "Your turn. What do you do?" What he saw was joy.

"I teach. Little kids, preschoolers. At a Christian school." She smiled widely.

"Sounds like you love it. Rewarding?"

"The best. The kids are adorable, but the parents can be annoying sometimes. Still, I have so much support from the other teachers and the director, Dana. It's a great gig." She searched his face. "I don't make much money, but enough. Teaching there fills my heart."

Alan took her hand and squeezed it. "That's all that's important."

THIRTEEN

Melanie filled her plate at the self-serve buffet with scrambled eggs, toast, bacon, sausage and fried potatoes. And a lot of fruit. She seldom had such an opulent breakfast, and she was hungry after the two hour walk on the Back Bay.

"I love to see a woman who likes to eat." Alan grinned around his own mouthful of eggs.

"Am I embarrassing you?"

"Not at all. Please enjoy."

"Maybe," Mel said as she settled and took another bite of eggs, "Maybe I can share a little about Natalie. But I have to trust you."

"You can. But please don't share if you aren't comfortable. And," he smiled, "you promised to explain about the candy-striped girls."

Mel held a napkin to her mouth to cover the giggle. "Of course. I forgot. Maybe I should do that first before explaining Natalie. You will have a better understanding of her if you know about us, our group. Let me enlighten you."

Twenty minutes later a server removed their plates and they were sipping coffee when Alan reached across the table. "Do you mind if I take your hand?"

Melanie smiled and reached back. "Do you understand our commitment to each other now? Even though I wasn't originally one of them?"

"Doreen's accident changed everything, didn't it?" Alan rubbed his fingers gently across the back of her hand. Did she feel the sensation he felt?

"Not immediately. But her forgiveness did. That and Connie offering her a job. Which turned her into an international model. A blessing for both of us." She placed her other hand on his and grinned sheepishly. "I practically begged them to let me into the sisterhood. It was a conversation I had with Cindy that convinced them I think. But that's another story."

"You girls, no you women, must have a zillion stories. Now what about Natalie?"

"She's actually really tough. She's had a few rough situations that she got over with a lot of faith. This one is the toughest, and we are determined to get her through it."

Melanie told him about when Bryce left Natalie crumpled on the ground in pain after an aborted sky dive. She explained how Nat went to Scottsdale to stay with Connie and Jaeda to avoid the men in her life and recuperate. She told how Bryce and Billy followed her giving her no relief.

"I went, too, to support her. That's when we got so close. Now we're best friends who share everything." She drew her hands away and placed them on her lap. "Not sure I should share what she's going through now. It's private."

Suddenly her eyes lit up. "I almost forgot about Emily's wedding . . . in the gym!"

"In Natalie's gym?"

"Yes. It was spectacular. Emily is a designer, a very progressive feng shui designer. Nat hired her to renovate the gym because she felt sorry for her because she was in love with Rob, Cindy's husband. Confused now?"

"About a lot," he nodded and raised his brows in questioning.

"So, Claire, a sort of self-appointed pseudo mother to Nat introduced Emily to her surfer son Nick. Of course, they fell in love as Claire the planner planned," she giggled, "and had a very unique and fun wedding at Nat's Gym. Did I tell you Nat surfs? Billy, Candy's brother, taught her."

"Now I'm thoroughly confused." Alan raised a hand to his forehead. "Let me think. Noelle is married to Braydon, right? I met him. Doreen is married to another Bill. Bill, Junior? His dad who everyone calls Big Bill is married to Vivian. And Candy is Vivian's daughter and is also married to a Bill. Nope, I remember he's called Will." He rubbed his brow. "Too many Bills!"

"It is confusing," Melanie said. "But Cindy is married to Rob, and Connie is married to Jaeda. They both have kids. You won't meet them because both couples are far away. But I know you'd like them."

"Natalie's never been married?"

Melanie shook her head.

"What about you, Mel? Have you ever been married?"

Melanie pushed back her chair abruptly. "Goodbye, Alan. Thanks for the walk and the brunch. Gotta get poor Lola tied up outside."

FOURTEEN

Alan paced on the printed hotel carpet scrunching his heels hard in it. Pacing seemed to be the order of the day. He had learned a lot about the Candy Canes, but most was confusing. So many men named Bill. Still he felt as if he'd learned nothing of substance. Especially about Melanie.

She was such a beautiful woman, a smart woman with what he called "presence." He couldn't put a finger on it, but she had it. She had charm and wit and warmth. All the things he'd longed for in a woman. But he sensed she would never be his. He could tell her heart belonged to another man. Who, and why? When she jerked back her chair and left abruptly, he knew. He had asked a personal question, and her behavior gave him an obvious clue. She either had been married or jilted. His thoughts wandered. Pacing did that. He thought about the burning sensation he'd felt holding her hand across the table. Had she felt it, too? Her long russet hair had fallen across her shoulders and it was all he could do to not reach across and touch it. She was wearing a blue skirt. She'd said something about it. Her prayer skirt? No, her God skirt.

He kicked the leg of the sofa and stubbed his toe. Maybe he should kick himself. All this prayer and God stuff was too much for him. He wasn't ready for it. Maybe Melanie wasn't his dream girl. But she believed in "God things." Was that why he reached into the nightstand drawer to pull out the donated Bible?

~

Should she take the call? She had left rudely without explanation. Why was she still so sensitive to Larry's deception and death? It had been almost a year. By now she should have put his lies and his death to rest. Especially since she'd made peace with his mother, Francine. Or when Vivian and Big Bill Lord hired her to be the live-in keeper of their home. Melanie laughed to herself. She doubted Francine actually kept their house as in housekeeper, cleaner. She couldn't imagine the frail woman scrubbing and vacuuming. Maybe dusting, lightly. Or entertaining her semi-permanent boyfriend, Carlos and his little dog Sam. She reminded herself she was grateful the Lords took Francine in and lifted the burden from her. All these thoughts sped through her mind like a cyclone. She pressed the button to take the call.

Why was Alan apologizing? She was the one who'd retreated in haste. He'd only asked a simple question.

"No, no. I'm sorry."

They sounded like two parrots. Laughing broke the tension.

"Okay," Alan finally said, "let's just chat."

Melanie was relieved. She really liked Alan, more than she had expected to. But she wasn't ready for a relationship. Was she? But why did her heart pound at the sound of his voice? Maybe she was just lonely.

"Just friends?"

"Absolutely."

"So," he hesitated, "I want to know more about you and the Candy Canes, and," he added, "why the striped swimsuits."

"Where should I start? Let's see. Mmm, not sure why they all bonded, but it was after their first big win as a relay team. They were only fourteen, high school freshmen, nineth grade. Wow, what a time lapse."

"A big one." Alan's laugh made her wonder why he cared so much about the women. "Did each have a special stroke?"

"Yes and no. I was told each was strong in one stroke, but they all could do every stroke well. Doreen did them all so well she was often the fill-in or sub if another girl was ill. Also usually the anchor." She stopped. "Remember, I was not on the team. I never saw them swim as a team. This is all hearsay from me. I was inducted into the group only a few years ago when I proved I could swim ten laps. How I wished I'd been part of them then," she sighed. "It was my understanding Coach Beckworth encouraged them to form a team within a team and let them choose a distinctive swimsuit; one that would set them apart. I guess he was so proud of them. That's when they chose the red and white striped suits.

"Why is this important?" she asked.

"Because you are important to me. I want to know everything about you. Sorry."

Melanie hung up frustrated. Why did Alan care about the Candy Canes' history? At least he hadn't asked any more personal questions again, like had she ever been married.

FIFTEEN

*N*atalie tugged the comforter up farther to hide the sunlight peeking in the shutters from her eyes. The alarm on her cellphone binged just before the clock on the bedside table played annoying music. Time to go open the gym. Maybe she could get Claire to do it. The woman loved to help and be available at a moment's notice just like a fairy godmother. No, if she asked Claire she'd have to explain why. If she told her, the woman would hover over her. Nat couldn't bear that thought.

She forced her feet to hit the carpet and carry the weight of her body to the shower. Showers always helped, didn't they? Turning away from the massive bathroom mirror she started the water on hot. First hot, then cold was her formula, her wakeup recipe.

When she got out the mirror was still there. Had she hoped it would disappear? She threw on a robe to hide her now almost perfect body. What was she afraid of? The doctor said it was just a few stitches to remove the imperfect cells. Maybe not even cancerous until lab results told. Was she afraid of the surgery or the results?

Or deformity?

Nat collapsed on her knees next to the tub and sobbed. She clung to the porcelain side until her hands slipped. Where was her faith? What is a breast anyway? Just embellishment on a body designed by God. At her age she would never use its main purpose to feed a child. Not to have a man touch it tenderly. She'd read about those things, but they would not be for her. Never for her.

She made the call. "Claire, would you take over for me today? Feeling a bit under the weather and don't want to teach a class with a runny nose." She was sure Claire would listen to her messages. She always had. She listened to Claire's returned brief "Sure" message and went to her closet. Pulling out every drawer she scooped dozens of brassieres in her arms. Blue, pink, black, nude, every color. Why had she bought so many? No longer needed. She bundled them in her arms and carried them to the bathroom.

~

Melanie tried again. Why wasn't Nat answering? Now she was worried but almost afraid to go alone to Nat's. What if she was so depressed she . . .? No, she believes. She knows that would be a sin. She would never. Would she?

She tried Candy, but she didn't answer. It seemed unkind to bother the women who were married, especially at dinner time. Why had she waited until then? She'd stayed late at school to deal with an anxious parent worried about Larsen her three-year-old not coloring within the lines. It was all Melanie could do not to scream. The mother was a CPA, and the father was a surgeon. No room for creativity in that household. She finally convinced the mother whose anxious eyes stared at her that many very intelligent children were also very creative, and her child was both. The mother clasped her hands and nodded with teary eyes. Now she was late to go to Natalie's as she'd hoped. What would she find? She was scared.

~

She pulled up to Nat's driveway alone. Why hadn't she found someone to go with her? Too late now. She rang the bell knowing it was a sort of courtesy since Nat had always said to "Come right in." Maybe she should wait a few minutes, just a few. Why had that irritating woman taken so much of her precious time? She would address the situation tomorrow with Miss Dana, the school's director. Dana needed to know about this stressed out parent. Maybe have a one on one about the child.

Melanie checked her watch. She had rung Nat's bell five minutes ago. Maybe she was in the shower after a long day at the gym teaching Zumba classes. Still she could throw on a robe or yell a come in greeting. Resorting to the semi hidden key she wiggled it into the lock. *Gotta get a new one made that doesn't need to be forced.*

She cracked the door and yelled. "It's me, Nat. Melanie. You here?" Mel knew she was since Nat's car was angled in the curved driveway. Strange it wasn't in the garage. Must have been in a hurry. Sticking her foot in first before pushing the door wider, Mel almost fainted.

Fire! She smelled burning.

She rushed through the kitchen and sitting room. The smell was coming from the bathroom.

"What are you doing, Natalie? Why?"

Natalie leaned over the bathtub stirring items with a big fork. She held a long lighted match in one hand and prodded the tub's contents with the other.

Melanie grasped her shoulder and pulled her away. "What are you doing?"

Natalie dropped the match into the tub and collapsed backward on the floor. "Burning. No use anymore."

SIXTEEN

*M*elanie dragged Nat out of the smoky bathroom and shoved her on the sofa. They were both choking. The shower had dosed the smoldering. It nearly broke her heart later when she picked through the tub contents of brassieres cut in half and mangled. Many from Pink and Victoria's Secret with scorched labels intact. Natalie needed prayer which she was getting from the Candy Canes. Maybe a therapist, too. But Melanie still didn't know what the doctor had said to her during the group's pizza party night. She remembered Nat finally emerging from the bedroom where she's had the phone conversation with the doctor. Her face had a pallor, but she smiled and did a thumbs up. Everyone thought the prognosis was favorable. Guess not.

~

"What were you thinking?"

Melanie propped Nat up on the sofa and shoved a pillow behind her head. She hated to be confrontational, but this was serious.

Nat hesitated too long. "Need surgery, to get the bad

stuff out."

"So? When it is taken out, will you be okay?"

"That's what they say, what the doc said. But I will have a mangled breast. I will be a freak." She collapsed shaking. "Just on one side." She looked at Melanie. "Don't you understand? I will be a one-sided woman. Just a half."

Melanie left reluctantly hoping the herb tea and tucking Nat into bed was enough. Nat seemed calmer and lucid. She promised she was all right. Vivian said she would come to check on Nat. So after calling the other women who promised to pray, Melanie went home and collapsed on her own sofa exhausted. Why was friendship so complicated?

~

"Sorry."

Nat's call woke her at five. She roused to grab her phone. Throwing off the sheet took some effort.

"It's okay. Most important are you okay?"

Natalie cleared her throat. "Yeh. I'm okay. Ashamed and embarrassed, too."

"Don't be silly, Nat. You were distraught, and understandably so. I'm glad I was there to help. Are you really okay today?"

The long pause worried her so she petitioned her Savior and held her breath.

Finally, Natalie sighed loudly and said, "Yes. Okay today. So glad you are my friend, Mel. Gotta go." The little red light on Mel's phone showed Nat had hung up.

Melanie didn't know how to help her except pray and be present. It was as the old saying went, a catch twenty-two. And a bunch of cut-up bras set on fire in a bathtub.

SEVENTEEN

*T*his time when Melanie rang the bell Nat answered and Melanie breathed a sigh of relief that her friend was in normal attire. "You look great!"

Natalie laughed and crinkled her eyes. "Just my everyday gym work clothes." She seemed to be searching Melanie's face. "Gotta at least look normal. For now."

Melanie hugged her and said, "You are normal. In every way."

Nat led her in by a hand squeezed tight. "I am now. Won't be soon. I'll be a lopsided woman." Melanie heard a laugh deep in Nat's throat that almost choked her. "Gotta learn to live with that. Maybe," she sighed, "someday I will."

Natalie stared at Melanie. "You don't know what to say. You are more scared than I am."

Melanie took the offered tissue and blew her nose hard. "Maybe I am. Maybe I am. So, what's next?" Wracking her brain for another subject, she said, "What about the restaurant thing you are supposed to got to with

Billy tonight?"

"Don't want to, but guess I should."

"Stop it, Nat! Stop picking your Kleenex into shreds. I know you're nervous, but Billy is a good friend. Who knows, maybe he needs your friendship, too."

"Billy?" She crumpled the tissue and shoved it between her knees. "He has everything a man could want. Success in his exotic car business, great family. Not to mention he's handsome," she chuckled. "Tall, blonde, buff."

"And?"

"What do you mean?"

"Well," Melanie cleared her throat, "he isn't married. As far as I know, he hasn't found the right one."

"Not me! Certainly not me! No way."

"How do you know?" Melanie asked.

"Gave him many chances over the years. Especially when he followed me to Scottsdale to Connie and Jaeda's." Nat leaned forward. "Did you know Billy taught me how to surf? At the Wedge?" Natalie looked down at her knees. "He doesn't like blondes. Especially with short hair."

Melanie covered her mouth with her own tissue. Was laughing appropriate now?

"Yes," she sputtered, "I remember you telling me. Doesn't that ring a bell with you? Like a challenge?"

"Yeh, it rings a warning bell." Nat stood up and the crumbled tissue fell to the floor. "Guess I'd better get ready for the food tasting extravaganza. He's picking me up in an hour."

Melanie picked up the tissue and tossed it in the trash. She let herself out, lonely. Maybe she should call the Alan guy. Would he be interested in the food tasting?

She found his number on her phone and dialed. Couldn't hurt to try.

EIGHTEEN

Alan was bored. Why had he extended his stay in Newport Beach past his three-day reservation? Nothing here for him except to visit with his cousin Rita which he still hadn't done. Well, maybe Melanie. But that would be crazy. In normal circumstances they would be three thousand miles away from each other. He didn't believe in long distance romances. Did she?

He picked up his phone on the first ring and tried to sound nonchalant. Yeh, right! Modulating his voice, he said, "Hello? Who's this?"

Her laughter gave it away, even if the caller ID hadn't. He stopped pacing and sat down on the sofa in his hotel room.

"Oh, hi, Melanie. So nice to hear from you." Was he being too obvious?

"Yes, I'd love to go. What do I need to do? I want this to be my treat."

"I've already ordered the tickets online. Wishing for a companion. You, of course," she added, and he hoped with honesty. "We can pick them up at a will call booth in Fashion Island. That okay?"

"Wonderful! I will pick you up in forty minutes. Just give me your address."

"Why don't we meet at Natalie's? You know where she lives now," she laughed a bit too heartily.

~

Alan pulled up just as Billy got out of his car. The two men stared at each other until both reached out hands. The shake seemed to confirm acceptance. But Melanie thought nothing was confirmed in either situation. She rolled down her car window.

"Hi, Billy! Hi, Alan! So glad you guys could meet again." She turned to Billy. "Alan agreed to escort me to the food tasting extravaganza. Long story why I asked him to pick me up here at Nat's."

"Oh. I would have been happy to escort you and Nat." Billy leaned in Melanie's open window close to her ear. "You sure you're okay with this guy? You can always change your mind."

Melanie squeezed her old friend's arm and nodded. "He's a nice man. Trust me."

Just then Candy showed up with Will. "Hey guys! How fun! We can all go together. Introduce us again, Mel."

"Love your shirt, Alan," Candy said grinning. "Tommy's?" His nod confirmed it.

"I bought it yesterday at Tommy Bahama's. Trying to fit in to the beach culture." He said smiling.

"Perfect, Bro." Billy slapped him on the shoulder.

~

The lines were long, but the three couples spent time to chat. After twenty minutes they got their chance at the steak tartare.

"Raw meat?" Alan's expression sent them all laughing. Candy was always dramatic and held her tummy.

Nat said, "It's fine, Alan. It's prime, and very tasty."

"Thanks, Nat. I will try it. Especially since it's prepaid for," he turned his head away after making a face.

Turning to Nat again, he said, "Are you all right? And how is the kitchen?"

Natalie's face went white. She grabbed Billy's arm. "I need to leave. Now."

Alan's face blazed red.

Melanie touched Alan's arm. What could she share? Not much without violating trust. So, she turned away and reread her ticket for steak tartare.

BONNIE ENGSTROM

NINETEEN

What was left of the group was huddled around the corner table in their favorite Starbucks. The food in the tasting had been delicious, but the waiting in long lines for bites was frustrating. Billy drove Natalie home. Her departure put a pall on the fun. Candy had finally raised a hand and herded them all for coffee.

Candy and Will had claimed the last large table, the one near the corner where they had all congregated to pray for Natalie before. When they saw Noelle and Braydon enter Will pulled another table close.

"Look who the cat dragged in," Candy snickered. "Grammy babysitting?"

Braydon smirked. "My mom tonight. But we did have to avert a fight."

"Actually," Noelle said matter of factly, "they are doing it together. Sort of in tandem."

"How does that work? Overlapping?"

"Exactly. That way they can visit and catch up with each other."

"Who gets the late shift? I can't resist asking,"

Candy said.

"I think they both do," Noelle said. "Lydia offered to come first, then Mom insisted, too. So, we struck a compromise. I suspect they will both be there when we get back." Noelle snickered. "We will be the ones to have the consequences of a spoiled child."

"Hey! Welcome, Alan. Nice to see you again." Braydon reached his hand across the table.

Alan extended his hand but his face was expressionless. Candy noticed.

"What's wrong, Alan? You seem hesitant. You okay being here with us?"

"Oh, yes, I really enjoy being with all of you. But I'm worried about Natalie. Aren't you?"

Everyone lowered their eyes. After a few moments Candy sighed. "Why? What do you know?"

"Not much," Alan replied, "but I know she's troubled, very troubled." His eyes scanned the faces before him. "I don't want to impose, but when I met her the other night, she seemed like a lovely person, but a troubled person. I want to help if I can. Sorry if I'm interfering. Just care, that's all."

Will leaned across the table and placed his hands on Alan's shoulders. "Thanks, Bud. She is special. Because of her Candy and I are back together again. Small gestures, big faith mean a lot."

Doreen and Bill, Jr. suddenly showed up. "We thought you all might be here," Doreen said.

"Glad you came." Braydon, always the gentleman, stood and gestured. "Sit. Join us."

The group fussed and reordered coffee. No one seemed comfortable. Just then Vivian and Big Bill sauntered in waving.

"Don't mind us," Bill bellowed. "Oldsters have different time schedules."

Vivian elbowed him. "Ouch!"

Everyone laughed. Until Melanie cleared her throat loudly.

"Maybe it's time to share." Her whisper drifted across the table.

~

"I sort of knew, but wasn't sure." Big Bill lowered his head. "Maybe Vivian told me and I didn't listen. Shame on me."

"I guessed. Wasn't sure." Alan closed his eyes. In thought or prayer Melanie wondered?

"How awful." Big Bill sounded contrite. "What can we do? Except pray, of course."

"I'm not part of this prayer group, but I've always believed in action. Doing things to help people in pain."

"Yes," Vivian said. "It's one of my favorite verses, Galatians 6:2. Bear each other's burdens."

"Well, I'm going over to see her." Alan threw his coffee cup away and stomped out.

BONNIE ENGSTROM

TWENTY

$\mathcal{N}$at's house was dark.

Alan rang the bell again, twice.

Finally, a slat in the shutters parted. He saw fingers, then a nose. When the door cracked, he put his foot forward, just in case. She stood there in the same clothes she'd worn to the tasting.

"What do you want? Is anything wrong? Has something happened?"

His hands in his pockets fiddled. Had he done the right thing to impose on her life?

"Sorry. Came to apologize. Can I come in?"

"'posse so." She ran fingers through her hair. "Don't stay long." She pulled the door wider, just a bit wider. "Why are you laughing?"

"Need more room to come in." He laughed again.

"Oh, sorry."

"That's better," he said leaning sideways. "Not much, but better."

She giggled and Alan plopped on her sofa with an "Aw."

"Make yourself comfortable. Like you did the other night." Was her tone sarcastic?

"I will, thanks. So good to hear you laugh, Natalie."

He heard banging and bustling in the adjacent kitchen. "What are you doing?"

"Coffee. Making coffee. Want some?"

"Maybe. Just had Starbucks, but yours is probably better." He rose and stood next to her at the sink. "Got yummy creamer?"

"Boy, you sure are bossy for a guest." She laughed again.

He leaned against the counter looking her straight in the face. "Guess I am."

"Why are you here? Did the others send you to check on me?"

"No one sent me." He hesitated, "Maybe your God?"

She turned and glared at him. "Why 'my God?' Isn't He your God, too?"

"Can't say, yet."

"Why? Don't you believe in Him? Tell me."

"Sort of. Grew up in church, but never made the connection. Wanted to, but wasn't sure He cared about me."

Natalie touched Alan's hand. When he started to move his, she laid both of hers on his, then laced her fingers in his.

"He does, you know. He loves you and cares very much about you."

"Why are you crying, Natalie?" Alan wiped a tear from her cheek. "Something terrible has happened. Hasn't it?" He wiped another tear and touched her shoulder. "Please share."

"Why would you care? About me?" She brushed his hand away.

"Not sure." He looked around the kitchen, then back at her. "Maybe your God, or your friends. Do you know they get together to pray for you?"

"Might have guessed. It's what the Candy Canes sisters do. We all do, for each other."

He touched her hand again and turned away.

"Gotta go. Just wanted to be sure you are all right."

He closed the door quietly behind him.

Natalie turned off the pot.

"He never had coffee."

TWENTY-ONE

"What is wrong with me?" The kicked leg of the sofa in the hotel room didn't respond. But Alan's toe did.

"Ouch! Gotta watch where I'm walking. Gotta get over this obsession with those crazy women. Gotta sit down."

He plunked himself on the sofa and arranged his feet on the matching ottoman just before his phone chimed.

"Blast! Why did I leave it across the room?"

Sighing, he rose to grab it right as it stopped ringing. He threw it across the room with gusto and laughed. Reaching across the king-size bed that took up over half of the room, he pushed the blue button for *Recents*. Natalie?

"Didn't expect her after our situation when I burst in on her." He addressed the mirror above the dresser and scratched his stubble of a beard. "Why am I talking to a mirror? I hope I'm not senile, yet. At least you," he said staring in the glass, "don't talk back to me or argue with me. That's a plus, I guess."

Maybe he should call her back. Maybe he should

listen to her message. Couldn't hurt. Maybe. It did seem odd that she'd call right after he'd just left her place. He didn't think he'd left anything but checked the nightstand to be sure his keys and wallet were there. Still, it was odd.

Retreating to his former position on the sofa, he wrapped a blanket around his shoulders. "Newport gets cold at night," he whispered. "Or maybe it's the AC."

After pressing the button to listen to her message, he dialed.

"Why are you apologizing to me? I was the insensitive clod who burst in on you."

"Because you seemed to care," was the answer.

"Are you crying, Natalie?" No response but a muffled choking sound. "Sounds like it. Please tell me."

"Can't over the phone." The choking sound stopped, but her voice was clear. "Come to dinner. Please. Now." Was it a command, or a plea?

"Give me thirty minutes. Okay?"

He could almost hear the nod, but the click was certain.

TWENTY-TWO

*T*he route to her house was becoming familiar. He could put his little rental car on auto if there was such a device. Why did she call him? Why him? She had so many close friends, and the Billy guy she went to the tasting with seemed almost like a brother to her. Maybe that was the problem.

She needed someone new and non-judgmental as a sounding board. That's it! He'd listen, be sympathetic, give her a hug and move on. Yes, she was cute, but not Melanie. Melanie had flair, a certain elegance and sophistication, a *je ne sais quoi,* one of the few phrases he'd learned during his three-day trip to Paris years ago. Pulling the keys out of the ignition, he laughed at himself. What was he worried about?

She opened the door wide this time. Instead of the jeans she'd worn to the tasting, she was wearing a fancy dress. Red! With sparkles on the skirt. Or was it glitter? Didn't matter. She looked beautiful, radiant and in charge.

"H – hi! You look lovely." Was that the appropriate compliment? He hoped so because she did.

She smiled a smile that glowed and reached his eyes. He felt heat creeping up his neck. What was happening?

"Thank you, Alan. So glad you could come." She pulled the door wider. He saw a table set with napkins and cutlery and a vase of flowers in the middle. Was he being wooed? Suddenly he didn't care.

~

"Where's Alan?" Candy dabbed a beige paper napkin to her lips and scanned the restaurant. The group was still sitting in Starbucks chatting.

"Don't know. I thought maybe he just went to the restroom," Melanie said. "He has been gone a while."

"Maybe he gave up on us," Will said. "We can get pretty self-involved."

"Perhaps he went to visit his cousin Rita?" Doreen said.

"That would make sense since that's why he came here," Vivian agreed.

Melanie shook her head. "I think he would have told me."

"Why? Do you have dibs on him, Mel?" Candy winked at Melanie. "He is a cute guy. Charming, too. Especially for a geek."

"Why would you say that? About geeks, I mean," Noelle asked.

"Computer geeks are usually dull, uninteresting guys. Mel knows, don't you, Mel? Like that Doug guy who comes to the preschool to fix our computers. Boring!" Candy giggled.

"Not fair, Can, to categorize them. And," she continued, "Alan is not a guy who 'fixes' computers. He has a very responsible job. High level, I think. Important." She frowned at Candy and said, "Besides, the Doug guy is very nice, very courteous and efficient."

"You girls are silly," Vivian said. "He probably had an errand. And, I think I remember him waving goodbye, but you were all jabbering."

"I heard him say something about being a man of action," Bill Junior said. "Wish I'd thought of that."

"You are, Bill, at just the right times." Doreen squeezed his hand and blushed.

"Learned it from me!" his dad announced loudly.

"William Lord!" Vivian slapped his arm with gusto, but her cheeks were flushed.

Everyone burst into laughter and Braydon high fived. Noelle pulled at his sleeve and pushed back her chair.

"Time to go, Mr. Rose Expert. You have a seminar to give tomorrow. And the grandmas are probably exhausted from changing stinky diapers."

"Aw," Braydon sneered. "To be or not to be. That's always the question."

Will leaned into Candy. "What are they talking about?" he whispered.

"He's the rose expert at the Sherman Gardens. Probably giving a lecture tomorrow."

"But the Shakespeare quote? I don't get it."

"She teaches Shakespeare at the high school. Thought you knew."

"Guess I need to get a life, Sweetie. Let's go home."

After all the couples left Melanie sat alone rubbing her thumb on the mythical siren design of the paper cup. Why was she always the lonester? Because she was a widow? Or, maybe there were no available men left in Newport. She tossed her cup in the trash and walked to her car alone. Again.

TWENTY-THREE

Alan couldn't believe what was happening, but he didn't fight it.

She tucked her fingers into his and led him by the hand to the sofa. Sitting just inches away from him she fluffed the glittering red skirt, crossed her ankles and pursed her lips.

"You look beautiful in that dress."

"Maybe you are just what I need," Natalie said softly.

"I don't understand." Should he? He felt like a fool.

She smiled, even glowed. "Should I wear dresses more often you think?"

"Yes. Absolutely." He looked at an art deco painting on the opposite wall and cleared his throat. "But you look great in sweats, too. Probably easier attire to wear to work at your gym." He cleared his throat again.

"Is something stuck in your throat, Alan? Or maybe it's the ocean breeze air." She smiled a radiant smile. "Happens to visitors. Even to locals during the June gloom. Although that's hopefully over."

He raised his face to sniff and was rewarded with the smell of garlic.

"Love the smell of garlic. What are we having to eat?" How blatant was that? If he'd been alone, he would have slapped his silly mouth.

She laughed again. This time it sounded like a melody. A little tinkling, then a crescendo. Then his stomach rumbled in harmony.

"You must be hungry. Should I tell you, or do you want a surprise?"

"I love surprises." He despised lying, but hoped it was worth it. Why was she being so coy?

"Come sit." She led him to the beautifully set elegant table. "I hope you like chicken."

The first bite melted against his tongue, and he felt his eyes pop. "What is this? It's wonderful."

"Just a simple Chicken Alfredo. Would you like more salad?"

Suddenly she clasped her hands at her throat. "Oh, my! We forgot to say grace. Sorry."

"No worries." He bowed his head with a mouthful of pasta hoping he wasn't expected to participate in the homily. What he heard, what she said, almost scared him.

~

Natalie had never been embarrassed talking to God, until now, until the prayer. Why had she asked Him if Alan was "the one?" Why hadn't she used the word friendship instead of romance? When she'd said that word Alan choked. On her perfect pasta, too.

"Ugh! I am such an idiot, Lord. Why didn't You stop me? Yeh, I know – free will." She threw the dishes in the sink with a clank. Alan had offered to stay and help clean up, but she gripped his arm and led him to the door. Thrusting a few napkin-wrapped brownies in his hand she practically shoved him out with, "I'm sorry. So sorry."

He had grabbed her hands with his free one, the brownies clutched in the other. He'd even said some saccharine comments. "Wonderful dinner, Natalie. So delicious. You are a lovely woman. And I love the red dress."

"Why, Lord, did I cry then? Couldn't You have stopped me, at least until I shut the door?"

She took off the dreaded red dress, crumpled it and tossed it in the laundry basket. Five minutes later she retrieved it, spit on it and took it to the big black can in the garage. That sales woman had been wrong. "Very enticing to suitors," she'd said.

"Well, not that suitor, lady!"

TWENTY-FOUR

$\mathcal{M}$elanie had given up. She hadn't expected a call from anyone, least of all him. She hesitated before pressing the accept button. Well, why not?

"Hi! Is that Lola I hear barking?" Alan asked.

"Uh, yeh, she does every once in a while." She rolled her eyes. "Dogs do that, you know."

Alan laughed a bit too loudly.

"Why did you abandon us at Starbucks?" Might as well get right to the crux of the situation. She wished he could see the sneer on her face. Was she proud of herself for doing that? Absolutely.

Silence

"Well?"

"I said goodbye to everyone. Isn't that when Will slapped my shoulder? Or was that earlier?"

"Don't remember, but you suddenly disappeared. Not a nice way to treat your new friends." That made her feel good. She hopped he was squirming. Maybe she should go on Facetime so she could see. She couldn't resist baiting him any longer.

"Where did you go that was so urgent, so important?"

"Remember that old phrase about curiosity killing the cat?"

"Got it. None of my beeswax. One of my Nana's old phrases."

This conversation, if one could call it that, was going nowhere. Just before she clicked the red button she asked, "Why did you call?"

"Because I care."

Click.

~

Alan stared at his phone. "Unbelievable. Just like that she hung up on me." Now he was talking to a silent device in the palm of his hand. "Ugh! What did I say? Do? Mmm. Does it mean she cares, that she asked what I was doing?" He shoved his fingers through his hair. "I hope that's why. I sure hope." Grinning to himself he remembered his granny's phrase, *Hope springs eternal*. He counted on that.

He went to the wash basin in the bathroom of the mini suite to check on his shirt. Sometimes he was such a slob, especially around a beautiful woman. Swishing the shirt around in the small basin of water he noticed the red stain was almost gone. He could use the hotel's laundry service if he wanted to pay the exorbitant price. Naw, he'd hope for the best. Or . . . would that be an excuse to call Melanie to ask about a local dry cleaner?

TWENTY-FIVE

"What happened?" Melanie tried to sound calm, even held her phone at arm's length, but Natalie was freaking out.

"My neighbor, I think her name's Gladys, wears a pink robe and curlers all day long, never met her before, banged on my door. Said I am a loose woman. Me!"

"Whoa, calm down, Nat. Why would she say that? Take a breath."

"She doesn't even know me. Never took the trouble to. Just stands on her porch and yells back at her husband. Sometimes she uses binoculars. I see her there every morning when I leave for the gym and when I come home. Nosy, nosy person." Natalie finally took a breath, and Melanie could hear sobbing.

"Goodness, Nat. Why would she say that about you? She doesn't even know you? Stop crying and make sense. Tell me what happened that she would say that."

Finally, after several deep breaths, Natalie spoke more coherently. When she did Melanie rolled her eyes and immediately started to pray.

"I invited Alan to dinner last night. You okay with that?"

"Uh, sure, fine. He told me. Sort of."

"He did? Did he tell you all? Like about the sauce on his shirt? That must have been what that Gladys woman saw."

"She saw sauce on his shirt?"

"No. She saw him take it off. The shirt I mean. When he left."

"Why did he take it off? Oh, got it. So he wouldn't walk into the hotel with a stained shirt. But he wouldn't have walked in bare, without a shirt, would he?"

"Don't know. He must have had a clean shirt in his car. I do that sometimes when I'm coming from the gym all sweaty and need to go to the grocery store, I make a quick change to look presentable. Lots of people do." Suddenly, Natalie giggled. "Funny, huh? She must have thought we had been . . ." Her voice trailed off.

"Oh. I understand now. That's not so awful."

"Maybe it is. It could be. The Gladys woman said she would report me to the HOA. As a woman of ill repute running a brothel. Can you imagine?"

"Surely the people who serve on your community homeowners association board have more sense."

"There's more."

"Uh, oh."

"After Alan left Billy came by to see if I was all right. When I didn't answer the bell immediately, he banged on the door yelling, 'Nat. I know you're in there. Open up. I'm getting desperate.' Gladys saw that, and heard it, too." Natalie took another deep breath. "Or so she said. She must have heard him or she wouldn't have been able to repeat it." Nat coughed. "How awful."

"Oh." Melanie couldn't think of what to say. It did sound odd, two men in a short time going into Natalie's. But people visit friends all the time. What was wrong with the Gladys woman? What is her problem?

"Got it, Nat. The woman is lonely. Maybe you should take her some of your special cookies. Or your special pasta sauce. I bet she would like that."

"Wouldn't that be an admission of guilt? Like I'm trying to absolve myself? She could turn that around to make things worse. Even say I'm bribing her."

Nat suddenly giggled uncontrollably. "I forgot."

"What? Forgot what?"

"After Billy left. Hic, hic."

Melanie clicked her phone to Facetime. Nat was holding both hands in front of her mouth. She looked like she was almost doubled over with laughter.

"Nat? You okay?"

"Yes. Hic. And no. Hic. But I figured it out. Why the woman thought what she did."

"Well?"

"Let me take a deep breath before I tell you, or I'll start laughing again."

Melanie watched her run fingers through her hair, straighten her shoulders and stretch.

"Okay. Now. Hope I can keep a straight face. I know you have me on Facetime. I'll put you on, too." Nat grinned into her phone and giggled. "Ready?"

"Waiting."

"Billy wasn't here long. About five minutes. Just to check on me." She paused. "I know I'm repeating myself, but I have to put my thoughts in order to make sense."

Melanie nodded encouragement.

"Just after he left Candy and Will came. Also, to check on me. Candy stayed in the car, so Will came to the door alone. I heard their car pull up, so I held the door open." She stopped talking and stared into her phone. "You know how sweet Will is. He's such a dear." Melanie nodded. "He gave me a great big brotherly hug. Right in the open doorway."

"Nat, you have to stop laughing. I can barely understand you."

"Oh, there's more, Mel. There's more," she said and burst into a spurt of giggles. Her cheeks were bright pink, and a tear made a trail on one.

"What on earth? What else?"

"Candy and Will pulled away and waved to another car coming up the drive. Guess who."

"I'm sure I know. And probably Vivian stayed in their car, too."

Nat nodded. One hand was over each eye now.

"Of course," Mel said, "Big Bill was his blustery self, probably yelling your name. Right?"

"Right. I'm sure all the neighbors heard him. At least she, the nosy one, did. Of course, he sort of started to push his way in. You know how Bill is. So kind, but not very subtle. Whew, need a breath."

Melanie counted about thirty seconds passing.

"Okay. I'm back. Vivian was in the car yelling, 'Hurry up, Bill. Don't take too long.' And I said loudly, I think, 'So sweet of you, Bill. But I'm tired tonight. Thanks anyway."

Melanie echoed Nat's laughter. No wonder the old biddy thought what she thought. Four men in succession within minutes of each other.

~

Melanie held her stomach and wiped tears of laughter when she clicked off from Nat. After a cup of strong black coffee, she sat down to make a plan. She would call Nat in the morning to share it. Maybe even call that turncoat Alan, who started it all. Of course, she would have to include the others. Nat would need them all.

BONNIE ENGSTROM

TWENTY-SIX

"You really think it would work?" Candy was howling with laughter.

"I wish I could be there," Cindy said, her voice laughing all the way from Costa Rica.

"Me, too," echoed Connie. "Scottsdale isn't that far from Newport. Maybe I could be."

"Stop laughing, Bill!" Doreen giggled.

"You, too, Braydon. It's funny, but not that funny. It's serious." Noelle was always the teacher. Melanie wondered if she ever put Braydon in a corner. Or made him recite Shakespeare.

All the Candy Canes were on a group call. Cindy in Costa Rica and Connie in Scottsdale both regretted not being able to personally be present for part of Melanie's plan. Jaeda offered to fly Connie to Newport, but had second thoughts when he realized he'd have to take care of the twins, alone.

Melanie was sure Connie batted his arm when she heard Jake the dog barking. Everybody laughed.

"So," Noelle asked, "what is the plan?"

"Uh, oh," Cindy said, "did you call Vivian and Bill?"

"Gonna do that now." Melanie paused. "Okay if I call Alan, too?"

"Sure. Of course." It was almost a group echo.

"After all, his shirt changing started the whole fiasco," Candy said snickering.

"Yes. He must be included."

"Gotta be there."

"He's the culprit."

"Put your plan into action, Mel." This was from Jaeda, the most rational of them. Maybe because he was a corporate business guy.

"I'll provide the flowers," Braydon offered, "from Love in Bloom. Least I can do."

"Got Vivian and Bill on the phone," Melanie said.

"Count us in. Stop interrupting, Bill." More group laughter. They all knew Big Bill always turned problems over to Viv, but he still wanted to be involved.

"Was it my fault?" he bellowed.

"Nope. But it sounded like you were the icing on the cake, buddy."

"Let's go! Let's do it." Noelle was getting impatient.

"I will call Alan now," Mel said.

~

Alan stared at his phone. Was she calling to apologize for hanging up on him? Well, he would be courteous, but distant. Until he heard the reason for her call.

"You're kidding." Wasn't she?

"Nope. This crazy neighbor really believes Nat is running a house of ill repute."

"Wow, poor Natalie. What can we do? How can I

help?"

When he heard the plan, he whooped!

"Count me in one hundred percent."

"I hoped so, Alan, since it was you who started this travesty."

"Not deliberately." Why was his nose twitching?

"I suppose not. But it's always good to think ahead before acting. Our community is pretty old-style, traditional."

"Yeh. The old *it wasn't raining when Noah built the ark* thing." He laughed heartily. "Let's rain on this biddy's parade!"

TWENTY-SEVEN

*M*elanie presented the group with several ideas. She had a favorite, but a vote needed to be taken. Cindy and Connie knew the Baywood community well, even though they no longer lived in Newport Beach.

"I remember Baywood well," Cindy said. "Lovely place but some, not all, judgmental people."

"Me, too," Connie echoed. "So glad Jaeda got that promotion so we could move to Scottsdale. More laid back. I can design clothing anywhere." She paused and gave a low chuckle. "I'm dying to design a wedding dress for Natalie. Just saying."

"Time will tell," Melanie said. "Time will tell."

She had shared several ideas. One was to nominate the Gladys woman as president of the homeowner association. Checking the Baywood Homeowners Association website she discovered the board voting in new members was coming up in two weeks.

Too late to put her on the ballot, unless nominations were accepted from the floor.

What about Gladys' house needing repairs? Melanie

looked up the violations. Aha, her gate was one, still hanging off its hinges. Did Billy, Alan, Will or Big Bill know how to repair a gate? Big Bill could pay for it. But that wasn't the way this situation should go.

Melanie reread Candy's suggestion. Or was it Will's? No matter, it seemed to fit.

Block party it was! Gladys could still be honored, maybe as the write-in candidate at the homeowners' annual meeting. Such an honor. Wouldn't she be thrilled! Or would she?

~

Alan stewed around the cramped hotel room and bumped into almost everything. Maybe he should make an appointment with a podiatrist. If only he knew one in Newport.

He decided to soak his foot and the offending toe in the hottest water in the hotel room. No big container to put it in. The bathroom sink would have to do.

He stood on one leg with a foot immersed in hot water when he heard the buzzing sound. He forgot to take his cellphone into the bathroom. How stupid was that?

Wrapping a towel around his foot he hopped into the living room to pick up his phone.

What he heard made him hop more. Had to be at Nat's in thirty minutes.

~

His was the third car in line when he pulled up. Two more came in behind him. He recognized Melanie's with the dent, and Billy's was easy because he always drove something unique and rare since his business was exotic cars. Alan wished he knew more about fancy cars, but working in information technology he didn't much care.

He was happy with his little Prius at home, and the Honda rental here on vacation was fine. Or was it a Toyota? Couldn't remember. Not important.

Billy was firing up the community grill in a Boss Chef apron. He looked right at home waving a huge pair of tongs in the air.

"Join me, bro," he mouthed grinning.

Alan handed over a container of pre-made hamburger patties he'd run into Gelson's Market for.

"Thanks, man. Never enough."

Alan slapped his head. "Ugh, forgot buns."

"That's okay. We have plenty. And," he added with a laugh, "some of the girls eat theirs lettuce wrapped. Saves calories I guess."

"Can't imagine why. They are all beautiful. The girls I mean." He laughed back. "Say, may I ask a personal question?"

Billy shrugged. "Guess so."

"Please don't get me wrong. I'm having trouble figuring out all the relationships. I know your group is close, especially the women. But," he shoved his hands in his khaki pockets, "what is your relationship with Natalie? Or for that matter with Melanie?"

Billy tilted his head at Alan and shook it chuckling. "We all sort of grew up together. In Harbor View Homes, a tight knit community, going to the same schools, having the same interests. Close families."

"In Newport Beach?"

"Yep. Some of us grew up on adjacent streets. Rode our bikes to school together as kids on the greenbelt that runs between the streets. Then drove our funky first cars to high school. Yep," he continued. "I guess you could say we have a family community."

"So everybody knows everyone?"

"Pretty much." Billy paused to flip a burger. "Why? You interested in Nat?"

"Not sure. Confused," Alan held a plate out for Billy's latest flip.

"Just know," Billy said with conviction, "be sure. Everyone in this group is precious. We protect each other."

Suddenly garbled voices erupted. "She's here! Our new community captain!"

Melanie ran to clasp the woman's hands. She looked surprised and confused.

Melanie was confused, too. Had anyone told Gladys about honoring her, even about the cookout? She kept clasping the woman's hands leading her to the community grill.

"Oh, that smells so good. I haven't had a good burger in ages."

Everyone clapped, and Gladys beamed. Until she looked around.

"Who are you?"

TWENTY-EIGHT

Melanie guessed it was up to her again. Why was she always the messenger, the go between? She remembered it was she who'd had the brief conversation with the woman in curlers telling Gladys that Natalie is a good girl. Was it just a few days ago? Seemed like a long time, especially since curler lady had recently accused Nat of ill repute. Melanie squeezed the woman's hands gently and took a deep breath.

"Do you remember me? We spoke last week when you were on your porch. About Natalie, your neighbor." The woman squinted at Melanie's face and finally nodded. But no grin, just suspicion on her face. At least it was a start.

"Well," Melanie smiled, "we, Natalie, me and our friends, wanted to get to know you better." Another nod with raised brows. "So," she dragged out the word, "we planned this barbeque in your honor."

"Me? Why me?"

Melanie looked around for help. Why wasn't anyone else speaking up? They were all chatting with each other and leaving it all up to her.

Suddenly Alan stepped forward with outstretched hands. Thank goodness for chivalry.

"Ma'am, I've been so blessed with these friends. I hope you will be, too."

What was that look on the woman's face? Anger, suspicion? Certainly not a greeting.

"You!" she shrieked pointing a finger at Alan's chest. "You were here the other night. You were the first one."

Sudden silence. All conversation stopped. Everyone was now listening. The humming sound of burgers sizzling on a grill was drowned out with Gladys' high-pitched accusations. Melanie couldn't move. She was no longer a go-between; she was a silent observer of anger and blame. She helplessly watched the scenario unfold.

Gladys looked over the group and took a few steps toward Billy who was still waving the tongs in the air until she jabbed her finger in his chest.

"I recognize you, too, so don't deny it."

Billy shrugged and remained silent with the tongs still above his head.

No one moved, except Gladys.

Will was her next victim. Candy clung to his arm and displayed her most engaging smile. As a recovered alcoholic Will was strong. If someone offered him a drink he gladly refused. But when a semi-elderly woman badgered him Will didn't know how to respond. Candy clutched his arm tighter and whispered in his ear. He didn't move, but Melanie thought she saw him shake.

Vivian leaned into Big Bill and pulled him down from his height to hers. Was she giving him an idea? Melanie hoped so as she sent a silent prayer up to heaven.

She was close enough to hear Vivian whisper in Bill's ear. "Be good. Make this right, please."

It was obvious Bill was next to be accused. The woman's ire was palpable. She was on a mission to discredit. What would Big Bill do when she pointed her finger at him?

"Shame!" she spit out. "Shame on you at your age."

Bill Lord reeled. Melanie chuckled to herself. Big Bill wasn't used to being spoken to that way.

To Mel's amazement he dropped to a knee in front of the offending woman. Melanie held her breath.

"Madam," he said, "I think you have misunderstood the intentions of this group. We are all close friends, all Christians of faith." He looked up into a puzzled face. "I see you aren't sure about us." She glared and her lips held a tight grimace of distrust.

"We planned this meeting. We planned it for you so you could get to know us. So we can get to know you." He looked up again at her face. It was somewhat calmer. She nodded with a feeble smirk. Was she accepting Bill's explanation, or gathering more fury?

"Also, we have an honor we want to bestow on you." Another feeble expression.

Finally, in a squeaky voice she asked, "An – a – an honor for me?"

"Absolutely." Bill's smile was wobbly. "Melanie will explain. Sorry, gotta get up. Old knees."

Vivian helped Bill rise and everyone heard a crack when he did.

Gladys seemed more composed when Melanie approached her again. Hopefully the idea of being on the community board of directors would appeal to her. Organized Candy held up a list the group had made and offered her some choices. Fortunately, Community Watch appealed to her. Perfect, Melanie thought, for a nebby nose.

Natalie came home from the gym and joined them in her sweaty clothes. Gladys suddenly ran to her and embraced her, then raced to her porch and swung open the door.

"Hey, Earl, come out for a burger and meet our neighbors."

TWENTY-NINE

Melanie held back a chuckle. Finally, they would meet the elusive Earl who Nat had dubbed Gladys' silent partner in crime. Very silent.

A semi-bald man in probably his seventies stood hesitantly on his porch. Gladys kept waving and gesturing to him, but he didn't move. He even left the front door open. A possible escape route?

"Come on, Earl. It's okay. They are nice people."

Earl tilted his head.

"Really, Earl Baby. Really."

Earl Baby? Now Melanie really had to hold her chuckle.

Melanie saw Vivian give Big Bill an elbow. At least he was closer to Earl's age. He hobbled to the other man on unsteady legs. Melanie worried about Big Bill's knee after she'd heard the snap when he'd stood up from addressing Gladys. Still he gave a friendly wave and stood on the bottom step holding out his hand. He played the heavy to the hilt.

"Nice to meet you, Earl. Please join us."

Gripping the handrail next to the two steps Earl tottered down.

"Sure does smell good." He turned to Gladys and asked, "Why don't we ever use this grill?"

She glared at him. "'Cause you were afraid it would combust."

"No, Glady, that was you."

Billy stepped forward and placed a plate in front of each of them. Gesturing to the table under the Ficus tree, he said, "Condiments are over there. Enjoy."

"Salads, too," somebody offered.

"Guess what, Earl, I'm on the community board. Isn't that thrilling?"

~

Melanie was exhausted. Mostly emotionally. Natalie had quickly showered and donned jeans and a tee shirt, then joined the group. She deliberately sat across from Gladys and thanked her for being a good neighbor.

"Congratulations for accepting the community watch position. You will be a very good one. A watch person, I mean."

Melanie noticed most of the Candy Cane group held hands across their mouths during that comment. Natalie kept a straight face.

"Gotta bring you some of my choc chip cookies, girl. You need to put a little meat on them bones." Gladys leaned forward and pointed at Nat's plate. "What's with the lettuce? You allergic to buns?"

"Say, Gladys," Nat replied ignoring the question, "I would love to give you a complimentary pass to my gym."

"You take seniors there?"

"Absolutely!" She gestured toward Big Bill. "Bill

Lord is a primo member. Has been for years. In fact," she said around a bite of burger, "I have a wonderful assistant, Claire, who caters to our senior members. Will you come?"

"Can Earl come, too? We go everywhere together. We're a team."

Melanie almost spit out her food. Such a team. Gladys calling the shots from their porch, Earl too shy to come out.

"Been together almost sixty years," Gladys offered with a grin. "Not changing that now."

~

"Go home, Mel. I will stay and help clean up." Alan pushed her toward her car.

"Thank you. Not going to argue."

Everyone had hugged, including Gladys. Hers was a bit stiff, and Melanie had been glad because the woman's perfume was overwhelming. Still, it had been a successful evening. Yet she was worried about Natalie who disappeared right before the hugging. Lola was probably whining to get out. Maybe a brief walk would help them both.

THIRTY

𝒯he sea air from the Pacific drifting over the Back Bay was crisp and refreshing. Melanie felt the moisture soaking into her lungs. The moon, divided almost in half by the cloud cover and mist, gave her enough light to stumble on the path. Lola tugged at her leash and Melanie jogged to keep up with her. What had happened at the cookout? Had peace been made?

She felt a buzz in her jacket pocket and pulled out her phone. She was grateful she was never without it, especially on the Back Bay trail in darkness.

"Hi. Thanks for staying and helping. How did the cleanup go? More importantly, how do you think the Gladys situation went?" Why was she babbling?

Alan laughed. "It all went fine. Better than I'd expected." She could almost see the smile on his face. "What are you doing right now?"

"Jogging, sort of, with Lola on the Back Bay. Why?"

"May I join you?"

"Sure. I'd love that, but how could you find me?"

"Are you anywhere near the Marriott Suites?"

Melanie looked up and saw the glimmering lights of the hotel. "Yes! Right below them."

"Stay there. I will be down to join you in two shakes."

Melanie paced in place to Lola's frustration. Fortunately, she had a pocketful of treats to appease the anxious dog. She heard the slapping of feet and gasping of breath and aimed her trusty flashlight in that direction.

Alan bent over to hug his knees with his hands and catch a much-needed breath.

"Whew! I'm not really a runner," he gasped. "Guess I need to exercise more." He threw strong arms around Melanie with a "Hi!"

"Alan, you're crushing me," she laughed.

~

Natalie collapsed on her bed and kicked off her shoes, the fancy flip-flops with glitter on the silly bow. The ones she'd felt forced to buy to prove she wore attire other than gym clothes and sweats. Sometimes.

"What just happened," she whispered to herself. "Is it over with that woman? Can I now live my life without criticism or being spied on? Did I really offer her free passes to the gym?" She closed her eyes and tried to envision Gladys in workout clothes. "And Earl?" She jumped up laughing so hard she almost choked. "That was not nice, Nat," she admonished herself, but still laughing at the vision. "But it *was* funny." Tapping her forehead, she thought, "I will put Claire in charge of them. She loves a challenge."

~

Claire always showed up early to pre-open the gym and wipe the equipment down. She hadn't been hired to do it, just did it. It was a thing for her since her son Nick married Emily. Even before that. Natalie couldn't even remember exactly when Claire showed up or how she'd become such a fixture in the gym. Still, she was glad to have Claire. Almost a silent partner. Almost.

Natalie clocked in, even though she didn't have to as the owner. Still she wanted the others to see she was dependable.

How dependable will I be after I have my surgery? How weird will I look?

"Hey, Nat!" Bryce suddenly slapped her shoulder affectionately. "How's today treating you?" Where had he come from?

"Okay I guess," she shrugged and opened her office door quietly. Maybe no one else would know she was here. It would be so nice to sit alone for a few minutes.

She rubbed her hand across her chest. It felt normal, but would it after the surgery? Sure, the doctor said it was minor surgery, just a few snips. Minimal pain for a few days after, a few tablets of Tylenol. A little tightening from the stitches, normal. The feeling would return and sensation would be back to normal.

Natalie wasn't sure what that meant. She had never been married, not even had a serious relationship. The only person who'd touched her bare breasts was her. Yes, she had been groped, mostly in high school during prepubescent dates. She remembered Barth Thompson the quarterback and laughed. What a klutz! Maybe they both were. At least he'd paid for the corsage and limo for the prom. She had worked weekends babysitting to pay for her gown. It had been worth it to slap him hard on his shocked face.

She jerked her head up when Bryce knocked on her door then opened it without invitation.

"WHAT? I mean what? Sorry to be abrupt." Nat felt her face heat up. She hadn't meant to be rude. She managed a smile.

"You okay? You seem distracted today?" He leaned forward and held out a hand, but she had put hers on her lap under the shelter of her desk.

When Bryce finally left after reassuring him, she dropped her head in her hands and sobbed. Had he believed her? Other than Billy, Bryce was her oldest male friend. She wanted to trust him with her secret, but he had betrayed her once leaving her lying helpless on the ground after an aborted sky dive. He must have known. Must have been the reason he followed her to Connie and Jaeda's in Scottsdale last year. To confess? To apologize? To declare his love? None of which he did. What if he hadn't known it was her lying on the ground? What kind of man was he to leave anyone lying injured? No, Bryce was not trustworthy.

Natalie did what she always did every morning. Shuffling papers gave her a sense of normal. She made piles, even put some in the cute containers labeled IN, OUT, LATER. She was feeling better when the door opened again. Why hadn't she put a sign on it saying Please Knock like Mel had suggested?

Claire burst in and swept forward. She smiled broadly and positioned a padded chair across from Nat's desk. "Glad I replaced the old chair with this one," she said with authority pushing her salt and pepper hair off her forehead. "Now guests can sit comfortably to chat."

Natalie nodded. "Yes, thanks again. What's on your mind, Claire?" She hoped this wouldn't be a long conversation trying to persuade her to replace her desk. The woman was a great help, but sometimes a bit bossy. And, Nat smiled to herself, Claire was really the only person who sat in that chair. Maybe Melanie had once or twice, but mostly Claire.

"I love the new people, the older couple." Claire gave a thumbs up. "So cute."

Natalie straightened her posture and hoped no trickles of tears showed on her face. Since Claire was so excited, maybe she wouldn't notice. "You met Gladys and Earl?"

"Yes. They asked for me, told me you suggested." Nat noticed a puzzled look on Claire's face.

"That okay?" Claire asked.

"Sure. I forgot. Sorry." She smiled weakly. "How did they do? Did they understand the machines? Were they dressed for workout?"

Claire held her chest and bent forward laughing. Gasping for breath she finally coughed.

"Yep. Dressed to the hilt. Most unique workout clothes I've ever seen. Might win a contest. Of some kind." She pulled a tissue out of her sleeve to wipe her eyes.

"Are they still here?"

"I think so. When I left a few minutes ago they were walking slowly side by side on two treadmills. Chatting and laughing. Cute couple." Claire dabbed at her eyes and said, "Go see." Then she started laughing again.

THIRTY-ONE

*N*atalie held her breath, and her tummy. She was sure Claire had been exaggerating about the workout clothes the couple was wearing. But laughter billowed up to her chest, and, thank goodness, she managed to contain it.

"Hi, there, Earl and Gladys! So glad to see you here," she said waving a hand. Claire was spot on about the clothes. Earl's flabby arms dangled out of a sleeveless hot pink top. His skinny legs hung below oversized green shorts patterned in orange flowers. The nylon shorts flopped sideways with each step he took on the treadmill. Gladys was attired in sparkles from head to toe. Nothing basic about their outfits. At least they had on suitable shoes. Actually, basic tennies, but for now they worked. Natalie rolled her eyes and held her breath and smiled approaching Gladys with an outstretched hand.

Gladys pushed the stop button on the treadmill and almost fell off. She clapped her hands and raised her eyes to the ceiling.

"Love it! Love it!" she repeated. "I feel younger

already." She looked around at the sayings on the walls and grinned.

"So affirming. The sayings I mean."

Natalie nodded. "Glad you like them. They are all Scriptures."

"What's that mean? Famous sayings?"

"Yes. All very famous sayings from the Bible." She gazed at Gladys' blank face. Had she confused the woman?

"Oh. Never read it." Gladys put her hand on Earl's. "You can stop pacing now, Earl. Sessions over."

"Really? I like this walking thing." He pushed his stop button quickly and Nat rushed to steady him.

"You okay? You almost fell off. Gotta wait for the machine to slow down."

Nat was disturbed that Gladys had never read a Bible. She had a God idea and rushed to her office while the couple was packing up their towels.

She spotted them almost going out the door and yelled for them to wait.

"Here, got something for you," she said thrusting a bag toward Gladys.

"How special. Thank you." Gladys peeked in the bag and pulled out some of the contents.

"A book? And gift certificates for more sessions?"

Natalie nodded. She hoped that was enough. She wasn't good at witnessing, but she could give gifts. She turned away and prayed that Gladys would read the book and that God's Word would touch her heart.

~

It was late when Nat got home. She had ignored the ringing and dings on her phone since she was driving. Ripping off her sweats she dumped them in the basket in her closet, took a quick rinse off and threw on a caftan. She looked in the mirror and laughed out loud. So nineties. From her one brief trip to Hawaii. Still her favorite with the bright colors and flowing skirt. Time to check her phone. The first voice message was from a vendor hoping for her to endorse his workout clothing. *No deal, buddy. I don't endorse.* The second call threw her for a loop. What was Alan saying?

THIRTY-TWO

"Why?"

"Why do I want to come over?" Alan's voice sounded unsteady.

"It's late. And the nosy neighbor might get the wrong impression." Nat did a deep breath to steady herself. What was she scared of? "Is it important?"

"I think so. Can I come?" Alan's voice was firm now. "And," he paused for a brief laugh, "Madam Nosy is now in my pocket. I am her new hero."

"Why are you laughing? What I went through because of you was horrible."

"Sorry, Nat. We all know the woman was wrong and fences have been mended." His voice now sounded more apologetic.

"Well . . ." she dragged it out, "maybe for ten minutes. But," she added, "don't park up close. I will leave the door ajar."

~

Alan shoved his foot in the door with a chuckle. "Just making sure," he laughed.

Natalie fake punched him on the arm. "Me, too," she laughed back. "So, come settle and tell me what is so urgent."

Alan plopped right in the middle of the sofa giving Nat no choice but to sit near him on either side if she wanted to chat. Maybe she should reposition the two armchairs, pull them closer to the sofa. But the extra-large coffee table was in the way. Oh, well, next time she would rely on her own decorating choices instead of feng shui Emily's. She punched a throw pillow and shoved it behind her back.

"Spill!" They both grinned and Nat felt her body relaxing. Alan was a nice guy. Cute, yes, but not her type. Pondering what she meant about that she wiggled her back against the pillow. "What's so important?"

He leaned forward to place his elbows on his knees. Didn't guys do that when they were serious? When he spoke, his voice was very low.

"Need relationship advice."

~

Nat clicked the double locks on the door and watched as Alan walked to his little rental car. When his car door slammed shut, she lifted a slat in the shutters and waved with her fingers. He beeped his horn two times quickly and pulled away. What had just happened? Why did he come to her about Melanie? Why not to Melanie? Alan didn't seem like the shy type, but he was inquisitive. She'd answered his pointed questions honestly, and as briefly as possible. It was not her place, never was, never would be, to reveal what Mel had endured. Best friends that they were, Melanie would never have been disloyal to Nat. Should she call Mel and tell her about Alan's visit? Or would that be a betrayal of his trust? Not once had he said for her to keep his confidence. Maybe he hoped she would share with her best friend? Natalie couldn't deal with those inner questions tonight. Too much was happening too quickly in her life. Tomorrow was the day she was supposed to have her so-called procedure. Melanie had promised to go with her. Why hadn't she called?

THIRTY-THREE

"*I*'m here. I'm here!" Melanie threw her arms around Natalie and squeezed tight.

"I thought you forgot."

"Forgot to plug my cell in so I couldn't call you, but my heart didn't forget." She wiped a tear from Nat's cheek with a fingertip and took Nat's hands in hers.

Natalie smiled weakly. "'So kay. Just scared."

"You're shaking."

"Yep. I know this is the time before the actual procedure," her voice squeaked.

"Yes, prep time is what it's called. Time for the nurses to take your vitals and for you to relax."

"Relax!" Natalie turned away and hunched her shoulders. "How can I relax when they are cutting into my breast?"

Suddenly she shrieked so loud that nurses came running and several people in the waiting room looked up. One woman held her hands over her heart. Melanie looked around. What should she do?

"Ma'am," a nurse said gently pulling on Nat's arm to lead her aside. "You need to get checked in at the counter." She led a dazed Nat toward the nurses' station and asked questions. When Nat didn't respond the nurse looked to Melanie. "Can you shake her? Pinch her? She has to answer these questions."

Melanie fumbled through Nat's purse and found the needed cards for her insurance and her driver's license. She handed them over the counter to the charge nurse with a trembling hand.

"Ma'am," the nurse addressed Melanie again while directing her nod toward Natalie, "Your friend needs to sit down. She's shaking. I will call someone to help." She pushed something into Melanie's hand. "Get her to take this if you can. Try. It will calm her."

Melanie led a quivering Natalie to a chair in the corner of the crowded waiting area, took her by the shoulders, pushed her into it and slipped the pill under her tongue. The sip from the paper water cup was an automatic reaction, especially for a seasoned workout instructor. She took a deep breath and raised her eyes. A hurdle crossed. She looked around nervously hoping no one would think she was drugging Nat. For a moment she wondered why there were so many vacant chairs. Then she realized few people were sitting; most were pacing. She sat next to Nat and held her hand tight. She was whispering Psalm 55:22 into Nat's ear when she felt a presence. Or maybe it was the scent of a delicate perfume. "Give your burdens to the Lord, and He will take care of you," a soft voice joined in. "He will not permit the godly to slip and fall."

Melanie stared into a face blemished with scars and eyes so blue she could have swum in them. Like the ocean. At dawn when it was calm. She thought of the time her friend Richard took her to Little Corona beach to body surf, or was it to paddle board? She couldn't remember, but she remembered saying, "How are we going to do anything but swim? It's too calm to carry us. No waves." Richard just smiled and said, "Wait."

She looked across Natalie to the person sitting on her other side. The dark face beneath the pale blue hijab was so scarred she wasn't sure if it was the face of a male or female. It almost looked painted with swatches of copper and smudged with charcoal. Then she heard the voice more clearly. And saw the beautiful smile. Suddenly the face wasn't ugly and scarred, but glowing with love.

"My name is Farah," the smile said. "Do not be fooled by my name or my appearance. I am a Christian. I know the Scriptures." Melanie nodded with her and smiled feebly.

"Why are you here?" Natalie screamed. Her sudden screech bounced off the walls and her arms thrashed the air. People stopped pacing and turned away. "Who are you? Leave me alone." She moaned and sank back with arms still grasping the air.

Farah and Melanie each grabbed a flailing limb firmly and began to rub Nat's arms. The warmth seemed to calm her, and she crumpled into the chair, sobbing and sighing. The two women stopped massaging her arms when they heard light snoring. Melanie gestured Farah to leave Nat's other side and sit next to her so they could talk more freely. Farah gathered her skirt and moved next to Melanie.

"So," she said, "you are wondering about me?"

"Yes, I am. But since the nurse said she would send someone to help, I assumed you were the someone." She smiled at the other woman and held open her hand.

Instead of clasping it, Farah embraced it with both of hers.

"You want to know about me? Am I right?"

Melanie nodded. "But I feel stupid asking you. Faith builds trust. And I believe in my heart I can trust you. I hope you won't be offended if I ask why you still wear your head scarf."

Farah lowered her head and smiled. "No, I am not offended. I am accustomed to being asked, even stared at and ridiculed. It is part of my life, my heritage." She paused and embraced Melanie's hands tighter. "It is both the way I was raised and tradition. Many Muslim women, even converted ones to both Christianity and the modern world, still wear the hajib. I can't think of a similar example for women in America, but I'm sure you have some."

"I wish I could, but nothing comes to mind."

"Maybe because you have led a protected life?" Melanie heard a soft sigh. Embarrassment?

Farah lowered her head. Her cheeks flamed behind the scars and she said, "I am sorry. I do not know about your life. I made an assumption. Bad choice and not Christian. Your eyes! Are you crying?"

Melanie touched Farah's arm and nodded. "Someday, Farah, maybe someday I will share. It's okay. I understand." She a crumpled tissue from her purse and wiped a cheek with it. Smiling, she said, "Please forget I asked you."

"No. It was a valid question, and I understand why. I will give you my personal answer, the reason why I, just I, wear the hajib."

"Thank you, Farah, but it was an intrusive question, and really none of my business."

"It was a honest question," Farah said. "Also, about time I answer it for myself." Farah lifted her hand to one edge of the hajib's scarf and pushed it aside. Melanie gasped.

"So," Farah smiled, "you see I have no ear here. Do not be shocked. I can still hear out of the hole," she laughed. "But it is better to cover and also to not shock others." She smiled again. "Yes, it saves many stares at me, but it also saves upsetting others from worrying."

"I am so sorry," Melanie said lowering her own head. "I am ashamed to have asked you."

"You must not be." Farah squeezed Melanie's hands again. "You were brave to ask. I respect that. You deserved the answer."

Melanie laughed suddenly, and Farah asked, "Why are you laughing?"

Melanie pointed to Natalie. "She would be so embarrassed if we knew she snores."

Farah giggled and gently slapped her skirt over her knee.

"I have some questions."

"Sure, go ahead."

"Your Natalie, does she not have a special friend?"

"You mean like a boyfriend?"

Farah nodded. "You are her only friend to come with her?"

Melanie put both hands over her mouth to stifle her laugh and gestured for Farah to come with her to a more private area around the corner where they found two vacant chairs.

"You are laughing. I am wrong?"

"Yes, but it's not your mistake. Let me tell you about the Candy Canes."

THIRTY-FOUR

The pill the nurse gave Melanie for Nat to swallow worked. She awoke from her mini slumber, yawned and smiled.

"Where we going?" she asked.

"Time for your very simple procedure, Nat. You are fine. Comfy? Ready?"

"Sure. Just a little nip and tuck. Right?"

Melanie nodded hopeful she wasn't lying. She didn't really know. She gave the nurse behind the counter a raised eyebrow and shrugged her shoulders. Did the woman understand her question? Must have because she responded with a thumbs up and rolled eyes above a Cheshire grin. How was Melanie to interpret all that? Then she noticed the nurse's nametag. Rita. Couldn't be, could it? She remembered the smile and the way the other nurse Rita had raised her eyebrows when she'd been admonishing the noisy group waiting for a birth. The hairstyle was different, but that was nearly a year ago when little Braydon Lovejoy was born.

She was about to ask, when suddenly a handsome

male attendant spoke Nat's name and reached out his hand. Melanie thought Nat might swoon. She caught herself in time, too. He was incredibly good looking. Maybe it was the uniform, and the large nametag. She placed Nat's hand in Adam's. Was that really his name? Like the first man on earth? If the earth's first man really looked like this Adam she suddenly wanted to go back in time to the Garden of Eden. She sucked in a breath and composed herself. Was she more lonely than she realized? Taking a cue from Adam's smile she hugged Nat and kissed her on the cheek.

"I'll be waiting for you, Nat. Right here."

"The procedure will take about an hour and a half, Ma'am. Plus, an hour of recovery time. You might want to grab a bite to eat. Or, give me your cell number and we will call you when your friend is ready."

Melanie pulled a slip of paper from her purse, wrote the number on it and passed it to Adam with a nod. His voice was so deep it could be described as throaty. Sexy? What was wrong with her? Suddenly she felt a presence at her side. She had forgotten about Farah.

"Are you all right? You look dazed." Farah's expression was as questioning as Melanie's mind. Where was her mind? Why was her heart pounding in her chest?

"Yes, fine. Thanks, Farah, for staying. Wanna get some coffee?"

~

The women settled into a remote corner table in the large hospital cafeteria. Farah placed her tray of salad in front of her, bowed her head and whispered. Finally, she asked, "Only coffee?"

"Yeh, not too hungry. But it is lunch time, isn't it?"

"You should eat. Your friend will need you when

she is finished. You need to be strong for her."

Melanie nodded and rose. She seemed to be nodding a lot lately.

After a quick sprint through the cafeteria line, she came back with an almost empty tray.

"A muffin? That's it? No salad or at least a taco?"

Melanie laughed. "First of all, I am a huge fan of anything carrot." She broke the muffin in half and slathered it with butter. "And butter, as you can see."

"I love anything carrot, too. Especially carrot cake with thick cream cheese frosting," her friend laughed lightly. "But I worry your muffin will not give you the energy to take care of Natalie."

"Gonna be bad, huh? Lots of pain? But won't they give her meds for that?"

"Sure. But I think she is stubborn. Will she take them?"

"Let me tell you about Natalie. If you really are going to be her help, her support system, you should know more."

~

After explaining about the Candy Canes, their almost twenty year friendship and commitment to prayer, as well as Nat's Gym and the many disappointments Nat had with men, Farah reached across the table and stretching her arms toward Melanie touched her face.

"You are such a good friend. The best." Melanie's mouth quivered.

Farah tilted her head to look at Melanie up close. "You are sad. I see in your eyes. You had great tragedy. Please share when you are ready."

~

Melanie sank back on the fancy bed she had paid a fortune for before Larry's deception. She had planned the bed to be their marriage bed. But plans sometimes don't bring fruition. She had almost tossed it out the window when she heard a voice. "Wait." Was it God or an angel or something inside her?

Maybe she would never know.

She pulled the eye pillow from the nightstand drawer and pressed it against her lids. The cooling herbs eased her headache. She fell asleep dreaming about Adam. Or was it Alan? One wore a pale green uniform and one had a blotch of red on his shirt. They shook hands. Too politely.

Her phone buzzed. Natalie! Screaming.

"Where are you? You promised. Adam said you promised."

Melanie fumbled. Car keys, shoes, water bottle.

"Be right there, girl." She hoped she sounded confident, and apologetic. The hospital was only five minutes away. But was she awake enough to drive? And worse, park in the complicated lot? She snapped her seatbelt and grabbed the wheel. Why wasn't the car starting? Oh, keys. Put them in the ignition and turn them, dummy, she admonished herself.

Must be losing it. So tired.

Her little blue car shot forward with a lurch and stopped abruptly. Big bump.

"I can't believe it. Again?" Alan raced to her car door and flung it open. "Are you all right?"

"What happened?"

"Same old, same old," he grinned. Then he saw her face.

"What's wrong, Mel?"

"Natalie," she mumbled. "Hospital. Had surgery. Supposed to be there for her, bring her home. Bad friend. Fell asleep."

"Come with me. We will get her together." Alan steered her to his car's passenger seat, belted her in and turned his keys. "Which way to the hospital?"

THIRTY-FIVE

Confusing. Hospitals were confusing. Which floor? What area? Then she heard the sobbing and the screaming.

"Ma'am," the stoic faced receptionist said biting her lip, "I think you are looking for the outpatient sitting room. Over there," she pointed.

Melanie and Alan raced toward the banshee sounds. All Mel could think about was how she'd let Nat down and how much pain Nat was in.

Alan held Melanie back by her shoulders. "Let me. Please."

Melanie nodded as he stepped forward. Would this work?

"You! What are you doing here, Mr. Stained Shirt?"

Alan laughed and knelt in front of Natalie. She cocked her head and yelled.

"Why are you kneeling? Get him out of here!"

"Not going anywhere, beautiful lady." He held out both hands to help her stand. "I want to marry you."

"Don't touch me!" Natalie jumped up and held out

her arms, waving them, beckoning to everyone in the room. "Can't you see he's a turncoat? He's the man with the stain on his shirt. See, see. Look."

Almost everyone turned to look at Alan and shook their heads. Melanie started to cry just when Adam rushed in. What was he doing with that needle?

"No, Adam, no. She is scared and probably in pain. Please don't do that to her."

"Sorry, lady. The nurse called me. Your friend is distraught." He raised the vial toward Natalie's arm.

Alan blocked him and the vial clattered to the floor. "I will take care," he said in a firm voice.

Suddenly everything was quiet. People started pacing again, but no one said a word. Melanie heard mumbled whispers, but no sound from Nat or Alan, not even Adam who had nodded and turned away. The charge nurse gave two thumbs up. Natalie sunk back collapsed in her chair.

~

Alan carried a snoring Natalie into her living room and laid her on the sofa.

"She needs to get out of this hospital thing, garment, whatever. Can you do that?"

Melanie looked at Alan and nodded. "I will need your help."

Together they carried her to her bed and Melanie began to undress her. Alan quietly left the room until he heard Melanie gasp.

"What?"

"It's just, it's more than I thought. The bandage is huge. Across her entire chest." She raised her face. "Why so big? I thought it was a nip and tuck. That's what she thought, too." She covered her eyes with her hands and wept. "I thought there would be a band-aid."

~

Melanie snuggled next to Natalie to give her warmth, and hopefully comfort. Alan crashed on the couch wishing he was in his hotel mini-suite.

At four in the morning Natalie flung an arm across Melanie's face and started yelling again and flailing around.

Melanie eased out of the bed and rushed to Alan to tap him on the shoulder.

"What's wrong?" He sat up abruptly with a dazed look. "She okay?"

"Not sure. Come see. She's wailing and flinging her arms."

They tiptoed into Nat's bedroom. She was hugging a pillow and snoring. And smiling.

They grinned at each other and Alan took her hand to pull her back to the living room where they could sit on the sofa together.

"I don't know much about medicine, but one of my friends is a pharmacist. I know from him that some meds react differently in people. And," he paused, "I think she's having a reaction to a medication they gave her."

"Why would they do that? Why give her something that could affect her this way?"

Alan shrugged. "Maybe when she filled out a form prior to her surgery she said she wasn't allergic to anything. Maybe she wasn't, didn't know." He looked Melanie square in the face. "Do you know? Has she ever experimented with drugs?"

Melanie stood up and paced the short distance of the room. Should she share? They had only been kids. So easy to forget. She didn't even know them then. Just hearsay.

"Well?" Alan asked. "Did she?"

She sat back down again and put her face in her hands. This was important. No secrets. Natalie's health. Lifting her face toward Alan she spoke.

"I didn't know her, or any of the other girls, when they were teens. But I've heard rumors, snippets of conversations. It's a no holds barred friendship, so I wasn't eavesdropping."

"Go on, Mel. This might be important." Alan laid his hand on hers again.

"Candy, or maybe it was Cindy, or maybe Connie." She shook her head. "Someone mentioned once that the girls, some of them, had experimented with smoking dope." She looked up to catch Alan's expression. "Just once they, whoever, said. Just once."

"That's the old excuse, the just once excuse," he said. "I know. Tried it."

"You did? Do you still?"

"No, not for many years. But it can have lasting effects in some people. So my pharmacist friend says." He looked off at the window across the room that was shining with new sunlight. "Do you think maybe she still does it?"

"I can't ask her. So long ago she probably wouldn't remember, or even deny it."

Alan nodded. "Twenty years ago. Right?"

"Yes, and I wasn't there. But I could ask some of the others. Should I?"

"Good idea if you are comfortable doing that. It could save Nat a lot of pain."

Phone calls were not an option. Starbucks was.

~

Natalie was sleeping soundly when Alan and Melanie tiptoed out. He drove Melanie back to her car, then followed her back to Nat's so she could have her car there. Fortunately in one of her rampages Natalie said something about over tipping the Uber driver. Melanie had wondered how Nat had gotten to the hospital and hadn't questioned it until Alan asked if she knew. And she hadn't questioned Alan about why he was in front of her condo when their cars bumped again. Too many questions to sort out.

After Alan left Melanie closed Nat's bathroom door, sat on the flipped down toilet lid and prayed. She laughed about being on a throne, but she knew she was on God's throne wherever she was praying.

She brought up Psalm 55:22 on her phone, the Scripture she and Farah had prayed over Natalie. "God will not permit the godly to slip and fall."

She knew and believed Nat was a godly woman. God would not let her to fall. He would always rescue her, whether from pain or medicine.

THIRTY-SIX

Melanie, Candy, Doreen, Noelle and Alan settled again in the back table at Starbucks. Vivian joined them with Big Bill.

"What's going on now?" he bellowed.

"Bill. This is important." Vivian gently poked his arm with her elbow. He muffled his ouch and Melanie laughed. Vivian was so diplomatic, sort of. A biblical wife, but still making her point without embarrassing Bill.

She reintroduced Alan sitting next to her. Bill nodded a greeting.

"I hate to leave her, even for this. But it's so important we pray for her and her health, and her recovery," Mel whispered.

Big Bill touched her arm. "Sorry, Mel. Tell us what we need to pray about."

Melanie explained about Nat's animated reactions before and after surgery. She wept telling about the size of the bandage.

Big Bill bowed his head. It was the most faith-filled prayer Melanie had heard for Nat.

As the group disbanded, barista Sydney nodded, winked and smiled. She knew. Her thumbs up and her hand placed on her heart gave Melanie hope.

~

Nat's door was ajar. Melanie pushed it open further.

"Hi, there! Where have you been?" Nat's voice was strange. Fake to Mel's ears.

"Are you okay?" Mel asked.

"Just fine. You?" Nat responded.

"Sort of. Sure." Melanie sniffed the air. What was happening here?

"I feel great! The nip and tuck did the trick. See!" Nat opened her blouse and revealed two wrapped breasts. Was one smaller? Hard to tell.

"That's great, Nat. How are you feeling? Any pain?"

"Not now." She waved a joint in the air. "This does the trick."

~

Melanie pulled the covers up around her chin. How could she, or should she, deal with the new Natalie? She, too, had experimented with marijuana as a much younger woman. It had helped her get through the loss of her unborn baby when she was a teen. It had been easy to get back then. Not now with more stringent laws. How did Nat get it? From whom?

Melanie knew she needed sleep. A good night's rest would prepare her for whatever tomorrow held. She tried to remember that verse about not worrying about tomorrow because today has enough troubles of its own. It sure did.

Alan's call woke her at 5:45.

"Do you never sleep?" she asked drowsily.

"Sometimes," he laughed. "Sorry. We IT people rise

early to get the techie jump. You okay?"

Mel nodded then realized he couldn't see her. Thank goodness. No way would she put her phone on Facetime with droopy eyes and tangled hair.

"Yeh. What's on your early bird mind?"

"Wanna marry you, but proposed to Natalie."

"What!"

"Remember when I knelt in front of her in the hospital?"

"So?" Mel rubbed her eyes with the sheet. "You didn't. Tell me you didn't."

"Did."

"Why on earth?"

"Just blurted it out. Like a way to save her." He took a deep whooshing breath. "Stupid, huh?"

"Uh, yeh." Mel rubbed her eyes again. "What was the first thing you said?"

"Oh, that." She wished she could see his grin. "Fallen in love with you."

~

Melanie threw pots and pans into her sink. Dirty ones, clean ones, ones with purchase stickers still on them, but she needed the clatter to help her think. What had just happened? Did she love Alan? Enough to marry him? She hadn't felt that kind of love since Larry. She'd never felt that kind of love before Larry. She thought she had when she'd succumbed to the fancy words that led to her pregnancy as a teen. She still regretted her weakness then, but knew her precious baby was in heaven. Praise God, he or she was taken by the Lord and not by her almost decision to abort. For that she would always be grateful. Someday they would meet in different bodies as promised in Revelation. She was sure she would recognize that child by smell or touch.

The banging on her door threw her into a frenzy. She was still in her pajamas, no shower, only teeth brushed.

Alan burst in. Had she forgotten to lock it?

"Get dressed," he commanded. "We are going for a marriage license." He cocked his head and smiled. "By the way, you look cute."

She banged one more pan, then grabbed Alan's hand.

"Sit," she demanded practically shoving him onto the red sofa. Red? Why had she bought red? Blue was her color. She sucked in a deep breath and blew it out so hard the red lampshade shuttered. She breathed again and sat next to him, but not touching.

"Please look at me while I say this." She knew she was demanding again, but he needed to take in every word.

It only took ten minutes to expose herself, to tell about her life. To tell about the baby, how she caused the accident that maimed Doreen for life, her crazy marriage to deceptive Larry, to tell all of her heartache. Alan had to know, to know how flawed she was. Only fair.

"We can't do this to us or to Natalie. We can't." She wrapped her arms around her chest, stood straight and walked to the front door to open it. Lola whined at her feet.

Suddenly she remembered. What kind of dog mommy was she?

"She needs to go out. You do, too." She said firmly and held the door open wide. Dog and man walked through it. A car started, its tires squealed. Lola came in. She shut the door and collapsed on the red sofa and sobbed hugging Lola.

THIRTY-SEVEN

The sun was blinding. Another beautiful Newport Beach day. June gloom had passed and the breeze smelled like the salty ocean it came from. Melanie hated what she was doing. Picnics were not her thing like Connie's. She wasn't fond of the beach, either. Yet she practically lived on Big Corona, one of the greatest on the globe. She thought of Cindy and Rob and baby Robbie living on the Playa Hermosa beach in Costa Rica. What a blessing they loved it. Living free from materialism and obligation. Then she remembered why they were there. To plant a church. Still, she rationalized, they didn't have the daily routine of nine to five. She hoped Mariners Church was still subsidizing them. Guess they don't need much.

She wrapped another tuna sandwich and pushed it into the cute basket Natalie had given her for her last birthday. She wasn't much of a picnic basket type either, but today it would come in handy. And Nat would be pleased she was using it. If she even noticed.

How would today go? How could she handle the

delicate subject? She pleaded with God to give her the words. Would He say, "Sure, here they are" or "Your call?" She hefted the basket into her car trunk. What made it so heavy? Oh, the sodas and waters and iced teas. Bottles did that. Bottles of the mind did, too.

Nat flung open the door, a grin on her face and a joint in her hand.

"Can't take that, Nat. We could be arrested."

"So stupid that something harmless and recreational is unlawful." She put the stub carefully on the edge of an ashtray. "Saving it for later. Don't want to waste."

"What about the meds the docs gave you? Surely they help."

"Made me loopy. I don't want to become dependent."

"But . . ."

Nat waved Mel's comment away and laughed. "Let's go have some beach fun."

~

They spread blankets and towels on the sand at Big Corona. Today the surf was quiet, weirdly silent. Melanie could barely hear it. She shoved a sandwich in Nat's hands. "Hope tuna is okay." Perfect time to talk. She hoped.

"So," she started, "how long?"

"What? The cannabis?" She grinned at Mel. "That's what it's called, you know."

"Yes," she said, but she didn't. "Worried about you. Do you do it every day? A lot?"

"Used to when going through the Billy and Bryce situations. It helped." Nat looked at Melanie with a frown. "You worried? Guess you said that. Didn't you know when we roomed together at Connie's in

Scottsdale? Guess not."

Melanie wrinkled her brow.

"So, all the times you took longer in the bathroom at Connie and Jaeda's . . ."

"Probably. You were so patient," Nat laughed. She took a bite of sandwich and spit it out. "Can't taste."

~

"It's not your problem, Alan. I don't know why I'm calling you." Melanie hung up with "So sorry," on her silent lips.

She really shouldn't have bothered him. Not sure why she did. She knew he would call back. Was that her plan?

"She what?" Alan's usually calm voice shouted. Mel had set her phone to speaker and laid it on the sofa next to her. Maybe across the room would have been better.

"She smokes dope to relax. Says it helps with the pain from the surgery." Melanie covered her eyes with her hands, so glad Alan couldn't see.

"Coming over." Just before a click she heard, "Now!"

The pounding on her door shattered her daydream. Alan hadn't wasted time. She undid the latch and was suddenly in his arms. He almost knocked the breath out of her. Gasping, she pushed him away. The expression on his face said sorry. Mel nodded and led them again to her red sofa.

"Don't know what to do." This time she put her face in her hands and didn't care if Alan saw.

"Nothing." He raised her chin with a firm hand and looking her in the face repeated, "Nothing."

"But you can't mean . . ."

"I do," he said interrupting her. "You can't make decisions for her, you can't lead her life for her, you can't control her."

"But . . ."

"You want to help. You are her friend, her best friend." He reached for Mel's hand. "It has to come from her, Mel. She has to want it."

THIRTY-EIGHT

Alan was always so rational. Maybe because he was a tech guy and he was used to putting things in order and following protocol. Trying to control her own emotions, as he had suggested, seemed impossible. Especially the ones for him. She mentally smacked herself. How did he know exactly where she lived? He had pulled up to her condo at least ten minutes away from his hotel. She hadn't questioned. Why? Why not? But he had done it before, done it the other night when she invited him. Had she given him directions then? Why couldn't she remember? Why was her brain so muddled? Did love do that?

Too tired to figure it out. She summoned an old friend's mantra, "God's got it!"

~

It was her turn, wasn't it? Tonight she would take care of Melanie. An imaginary balloon saying INDULGE hovered above her head. She grasped at it.

She opened all the fun stuff she had ordered last month from ULTA for softening her hands and feet. The eye and face masks, too. But first a decadent bubble bath.

"I deserve it!" Melanie touched a toe into the bubbles and sighed. "Total relaxation, total indulgence."

She sunk up to her neck and heard the brr of her cellphone.

"Drat! Forgot to turn the phone off! I will ignore it. This is my night, my much needed treat."

Sinking low into the bubbles she paraphrased verse 22 in Psalm 55. "He will not let the godly slip and fall." I hope that's me, too.

When her skin started to pucker, she stepped out and wrapped herself in softness. She loved her thirsty white towels. Tossing one aside she glared at her face in the mirror, grimaced and spread goo all over her cheeks. And laughed. Where did those wrinkles come from? Powdering and stretching and praying helped. But how would Natalie get help?

"I don't know what to do, Lord. Don't know how to help." She waited for an answer, but none came.

Her phone rang again. This time she reluctantly answered.

"Coming over." He hung up before she could respond.

~

Alan was a man of his word. At least about coming over. Her doorbell chimed within minutes.

Melanie had towel-dried her hair, spritzed cologne, pulled on sweats, quickly did the eyebrow thing and fake grinned.

"Wow, you look gorgeous! Did I interrupt anything?"

Mel bit her lip. Why were men so clueless?

"Sort of, not really," she lied.

"My vacation is almost over. Need to finish some stuff. You understand?"

She shrugged her shoulders. Would that be enough?

"What? You don't believe me?"

"Should I? Your declaration of love seemed very casual."

"Melanie," he said embracing her small hands in his, "I say what I mean, and I mean what I say. Understand? I am a man of my word."

She whispered. "I hope so, Alan. I don't know if I can bear being deceived again."

~

After Alan left she drained the tub. She'd forgotten to in haste. "Can I drain my heart, too?" she pleaded with God.

Time for a Candy Cane intervention. One for her, not for Natalie.

Alan had kissed her on the cheek and squeezed her hands, tightly. His gestures had left her more confused. It had only been slightly under a year since Larry had died. More since he'd deceived her. Then her attorney and friend Randi had suggested a grief group. Grief was so personal. Some of her Candy Cane friends attended with her placing their hands on her drooping shoulders. But nothing had helped as much as prayer.

She clung to Scripture. "God is my refuge, my strength. I can do all things in Christ."

The gurgling of the tub emptying aroused her from her knees. She called Alan.

"Please come back, if you are willing."

THIRTY-NINE

She turned the doorknob. Alan burst in and wrapped his arms around her.

"I made a huge mistake." Alan's voice cracked and his face contorted.

"I don't understand. Do you not want to marry me?"

His laughter startled Melanie. What was wrong with this scenario?

"No, no! I do want to marry you, Melanie. Only you," he said bowing his face in his hands. "I just don't want to marry Natalie."

"But you proposed."

"Stupidly. In a moment to give her hope."

Melanie shook her head. "I have been proposed to twice in my life. Neither turned out good in the end." She bowed her head and whispered. "Nat is a wonderful person who is going through a scary situation." She looked up at Alan's face. "She doesn't deserve another disappointment. Not now. So, Alan, say what you mean and mean what you say."

~

The mini-suite was becoming too much like home

to Alan. He even tried to rearrange the furniture. Didn't help. Only so much room in a mini room.

Making decisions was his strong point. Time to make one for himself and two people he loved.

Her phone rang too long. Maybe she wouldn't answer and he'd be off the hook, so to speak. He chuckled at his own silliness. Nine rings. Time to hang up, then . . .

"Hi, Alan." She obviously saw the caller ID.

"Coming over. Need to explain. Leave door open, please."

She did. Dressed in the red dress, she sighed and led Alan by the hand to the sofa. She ran her hands over the bouffant skirt laughing. But she knew the laugh wasn't genuine. His blank face said he did, too. "Sorry it's wrinkled. Almost tossed it after the other night." She managed a wobbly smile. "I guess I had hoped."

The expression on his face told it all. He wasn't hers.

"Not happening, right? Bad proposal, no wedding?"

Alan nodded.

~

Natalie hung the wrinkled red dress in her closet on the padded silk hanger. What was a dress anyway? Just a garment, a temporary costume. Venus, the saleswoman, implied it was a symbol of hope. Especially because of its low-cut neckline to reveal appealing cleavage to attract the opposite sex. Well, no more cleavage for Natalie. Unless half a cleavage counted.

Time to be brave, to take off the bandage. Should she stand in front of the big mirror in the bathroom or not look and hold the hand mirror up after?

"Can't do it alone. Mel, come please." She clicked off her phone and hoped.

FORTY

Melanie shook and prayed the entire drive to Nat's. What was she afraid of? What was under the bandage neither of them had seen? What would be Natalie's reaction, or hers?

The door was ajar, as if someone else had just left. Her mind churned, then it computed. Alan. He said he wanted to make it up to Natalie for proposing impromptu to her. Had he?

She hurried in to embrace Natalie and stumbled over a pile of red chiffon, or was it silk? With sparkles and glitter. What had happened? Fearful of what might have happened Mel rushed to Natalie and wrapped arms around her. "What did he say? What did he do?"

Nat looked at her with raised brows. "Nothing. Perfect gentleman. Doesn't want to marry me. Said sorry. Mistake."

"That's all? You okay with that?"

"Guess so. Same old same old."

Melanie picked up the mound of fabric and shook it. "This is beautiful. Where did it come from?"

"It's my 'special dress', a dress to entice suitors. At least that's what the salesgirl said." Natalie sank on the edge of her bed. "Big lie, huh? She said red always seduces them. Or something like that." She wiped a tear with the corner of her sheet and chuckled. "A two-hundred-dollar sales pitch. So stupid. Me, I mean." She laughed again. "She was just doing her job. But I forgot who I was. Alan wasn't my type. Too proper."

Melanie was at a loss for words, so she took action.

"Let's pull the bandage off." Melanie found the end of it on Nat's back and tugged.

~

"Oh."

"Oh."

"Not as bad as I thought."

"Not nearly."

"I still have a breast. Don't I?"

"Sure do."

The women hugged, laughed and poured glasses of sparkling apple cider.

"Fake champagne!" Nat said. "I thought I had the real stuff somewhere."

"No matter. The bubbles tickle my tongue." Melanie laughed again and hugged Nat nestling her head in the other woman's shoulder. "Feels so good!"

Natalie pulled back. "Why doesn't it?" She crumpled a tissue and wiped her nose. "Still scared. Why?"

"Because . . . "she tried to think of every reason. "You are human? Maybe your faith is shaky? Stress? You are human."

Nat ran to her bedroom. The door slammed. Melanie could hear sobbing. Her heart ached, but she didn't know what to do.

She petitioned her Lord. She kept hearing the word, "Wait."

She let herself out silently closing the door and called Alan.

FORTY-ONE

𝒜lan held her tight.

"Don't know what to do." She buried her face in his shoulder.

"Nothing. Maybe prayer," he whispered.

"Maybe? Prayer is my anchor."

She felt his arms still wrapped firmly around her and looked up into his face. "You starting to pray?"

"Maybe."

"Why?"

"You. Your faith. Still learning."

~

"I need a Candy Cane group prayer." She called all the others and sat waiting in the corner table at Starbucks.

Vivian and Big Bill were first to come. The others straggled in. Candy and Will, Doreen and Bill, Jr. and finally Noelle and Braydon. Alan tried to slide in quietly, but all heads turned to him.

"You getting this, Alan?" Candy asked.

"Can I help?" Big Bill offered his hand.

"He's a good prayer pray-er." Vivian said.

Alan grasped Big Bill's hand' nodded to everyone and grinned. Melanie hoped his smile said it all.

"But," he said, "I don't feel complete yet." He scanned all the faces around the small table. "Need something more." His hesitation drew confusion. "Need a special prayer for . . . I guess faith. For me."

Everyone bowed their heads. Big Bill started to speak. "Dear Lord . . ."

Suddenly Sydney the barista raised her hands and whispered loudly. "Last woman on the mountain."

"I am here." Natalie announced.

~

Everyone stood up. All the men pushed their chairs aside gesturing for Natalie to sit. Instead she grabbed a chair from another table and pushed it between Noelle and Braydon. Everyone sat back down with blank faces.

"Now, what's all this about? Me?"

Candy bit her lip. Will gestured a hands down wave the other men followed. Vivian squeezed Big Bill's arm so hard he winched. Melanie's face blanched. Alan stood.

"I know you all know her as your friend Natalie. But I want to introduce the new Natalie, the brave Natalie, the overcoming Natalie." He lifted her hands in both of his and guided her to stand.

"This lady," he continued smiling down at her, "this precious woman has endured fear and ridicule and pain, both physical and emotional. You all know about the Gladys situation." Everyone laughed.

Alan wiped a pretend stain off his shirt and chuckled. "Whew. Got it off!"

Everyone laughed again. Vivian pulled a tissue from

her sleeve and dabbed her eyes. Noelle winked at Braydon, and Will tilted Candy's chin with a finger and planted a kiss. Melanie's phone chimed with two calls at once.

"Are we too late?" Cindy asked.

"We were changing diapers. But we are here now," Connie announced.

Everyone laughed again. Melanie pushed the buttons on her phone.

"It's fine Con and Cindy. Perfect timing. Did you hear what Alan said?"

"Yes. Yes. Couldn't respond in time," Connie said. "Me neither," Cindy echoed.

The whole group could hear Alan's whooshing breath. Still holding Natalie's hand he sat down. Big Bill finally said the prayer for Alan to invite Jesus into his heart.

~

Alan followed Natalie home. Both were surprised another car was in the drive. He got out of his car and held her hand to protect her, in case. Of what?

The door swung open to arms spread wide.

"Remember me, Natalie? I am Farah. I will be with you through everything."

Natalie crumbled into Farah's arms and wept.

"It is going to be okay, Natalie. We will get through this together." She smiled gently and led Natalie by the hand. "I promise."

FORTY-TWO

Alan pranced around the mini-suite and kicked everything he could. Every table leg, every sofa leg, every chest of drawers and both nightstands. He wanted his toe to hurt big time. He'd done it again. He'd messed up his life and his future. No mystery there.

"I am a screwup!"

Toe aching, he finally sat on the mini-sofa, propped his foot on the glass coffee table and pressed his head in his hands. "I know I should feel something more. Aren't I suppose to feel elation and excitement? Isn't the world supposed to see me as a different person glowing with Your light?"

~

Melanie twiddled her thumbs. Prayer always helped, but no words came. She remembered Jesus' promise that the Holy Spirit would groan for her when she couldn't find the words. The only groaning she heard was Lola whining for her dinner.

She put the metal bowl down and Lola pranced, even did her ballet performance. The bowl was empty in three minutes. Melanie's heart was empty, too.

Did Alan really accept Christ as his Savior when Big Bill said the prayer? She tried to remember. Had she looked at Alan's face, heard his voice? It was all such a blur. Everyone clapping and hugging and embracing Alan's hands. When her turn came his hands were ice cold and his face was blank. It was time to call him.

~

Keep it simple she told herself twice. Well, maybe three times. She touched the little phone icon above the word audio. His phone rang. "Hello, this is Alan. Sorry I missed you. Please leave a message." Click. Why hadn't he answered?

Melanie wasn't a pacer. But she remembered Alan telling her how he paced to center himself and to calm. Couldn't hurt. She also remembered he told her he kicked the furniture. For what? To make a statement about his frustration? Certainly not to deliberately hurt his foot. Still, worth a try. Couldn't hurt. Or maybe it could.

"Ow! Ouch!" Trying was believing. But not helping. Shaking her foot hard to bring back circulation she grabbed her car keys. Nothing like in person contact. She dialed again. Maybe this time he would listen.

"Coming up. What is your room number?"

FORTY-THREE

She rapped relentlessly on the door to Number 713. Finally, it cracked open.

"Shh. Neighbors will complain."

"Don't care. This is ridiculous! And, yes, I'm angry!"

"Me, too," he said as he led her to an overstuffed chair. "Sit. Please."

Melanie tucked the folds of her blue skirt under her legs and crossed her ankles. When she found her voice her anger almost seemed to spin around the room and slap Alan in the face. He jerked back. Did her fury really affect him?

"Who, I repeat, who did you think you were walking out on? Taking Nat home? Acting like accepting the Lord was no big deal?" She couldn't stop. "We all prayed for you. So hard, so sincerely. What happened?"

Alan shook his head, sat on the arm of the opposite chair and covered his face. "Don't know. Didn't feel it."

"But you said you did. Why?"

"Because I was supposed to?"

"Alan," Melanie took a long breath. "Do you believe there is a God?"

He nodded.

"Do you believe in an afterlife?"

He nodded.

"Do you believe . . . oh, heck, what do you believe, Alan?"

~

She took him to Pastor Lyn. The kindest, most understanding person she could think of to explain faith to him. Pastor Terry would have been great, but they would have bonded and had an intellectual smart-man-to-smart-man talk. Alan needed the sensitivity of a woman, a motherly woman. Since he'd been in Newport most of his relationships had been with women. Mostly her and Natalie. Even crazy Gladys.

Melanie ushered Alan in and still wondered why the door opened out instead of in as most entry doors do. She smiled as she introduced them.

Lyn gestured for Alan to sit. But before he could she took his hands. Her warmth and her smile did it all. Melanie left them alone and sat in her car to wait. This meeting needed to be private.

The weather was getting colder. No more summer. Mel turned off the AC in her humming car and pulled her sweater around her shoulders to ward off the chill. She sat in silence, no praise music from the car radio to soothe her. She wanted to be totally aware and, in the moment, when . . .. When what? When Alan appeared looking . . . How?

Did she love him? Like she had loved Larry? Would it matter if he hadn't really accepted the Lord? How would that impact their relationship? Could she even love again without reservation and fear? What if Alan wasn't what he said he was and betrayed her like Larry had? She felt sure he was a genuine IT person, and probably worked for the government since he had high clearance. Or at least he'd said that. Maybe she should ask for proof. She hadn't needed to do that with Larry because she saw him many times at his security post. But it had obviously meant nothing about his morality since it had given him the opportunity to steal. Before she could question herself further, she heard a woosh of air through her cracked car window.

The door to the church office swung open outward and was pushed closed with a thunk. Alan stood for a moment. His tall figure was face up, gazing at the blue cloudless sky, brown hair ruffled by the soft wind. Melanie's heart lurched. He looked so . . . cute. So boyish. So real.

Suddenly he raised his arms, grinned and did an impromptu shuffle. Melanie was tempted to jump out and embrace him. Instead she clicked the lock to open the passenger door. She squeezed his hand and smiled and started the car. A thank you prayer was on her lips.

FORTY-FOUR

Gladys banged on Natalie's door. Nat peeked out of the shutters. If it had been anyone else, she would have ignored it. But still not sure about the other woman's intentions after so many accusations, she opened the door wide with a fake grin even wider.

"Good morning, neighbor! What brings you here?" Nat stood to her full five-foot six height and composed herself. "Coffee?" Nat filled a mug and handed it to Gladys. Thank goodness she'd made a big pot. Maybe she'd had a feeling she should.

"Lovely. Thank you." Gladys pushed her way in and settled on a stool at the counter. She pulled her fluffy pink robe closer to her chest. "Sorry not dressed properly." She fiddled with her hands and looked down. "Worried about you."

"Oh. How kind, but why?"

"Just a feeling." Gladys waved the mug in the air. "You got more cream?"

Natalie bit the smile on her lip and poured cream in Gladys' cup. She sat across from the other woman and cupped her hands around her own mug. "So, share, please."

"Oh, that." The bodice of the pink robe got folded over by a nervous hand. The other hand tugged at a plastic curler in fluffy hair. When the curler fell out the hand grabbed it and shoved it in a pocket.

"Yes?" Natalie was more than curious now. Gladys was nervous and not confrontational, but obviously wanted to say something. "What did you want to share, Gladys? You said you were worried about me."

"Oh, that," she repeated. "Maybe nothing. Should go," she said and stood up.

"Don't go yet, please." Natalie touched her hand. "Have some more coffee."

"Well, maybe." Gladys held up her cup. "Is there more cream?"

"Sure is," Nat chuckled. "Now what has been bothering you about me?" She cocked her head and smiled at the woman. "You came over to tell me. Don't you think I deserve to know?"

Gladys fiddled with her fake fingernails and stirred her coffee again. When she raised her head, she stared at the morning sun coming in the window behind Nat and blinked. Finally, she spoke in a shaky voice.

"Probably silly. Probably not important. Maybe," she sighed, "a figerment, or whatever that is, of my imagination." She looked directly at Natalie. "You okay?"

Nat nodded, then burst into tears.

"What, Sweetie, what?" Gladys rushed around the counter to embrace Nat and held her tight.

Nat wiped her face with a fist. "Cancer scare. Breast cancer. Pink scare. What gave you a clue?"

"The book." Gladys nodded. "The book you gave me."

"The Bible?"

"Opened it randomly. Came upon Psalms, or is it Psalm?, five five. Maybe I mean fifty-five." She looked at Natalie for confirmation. Natalie nodded and said "Go on. What did you read?"

"I think twenty-two. Something about the godly will not slip and fall." She stepped back and twisted her hands. She spoke quietly, almost in a whisper. "Maybe silly, but from knowing you better I think you are godly, or at least blessed. Your face," she rattled on, "popped into my head. Made me worry about you. Haven't prayed for many years. Prayed for you." She hugged Nat again. "Now I know why."

Nat sent Gladys home with more cream in her coffee and the mug and a hug. Then she called Melanie and Farah.

BONNIE ENGSTROM

FORTY-FIVE

*M*elanie shouted into her phone.

"Do you know what this means? You witnessed. You are part of the Great Commission. God is using you."

Nat laughed. "Calm down, Mel. I get it. Yes, I am thrilled Gladys is reading the Bible I gave her. I pray she doesn't misunderstand or misinterpret." Nat whooshed a sigh. "She didn't say she accepted Christ. She's just worried about me."

"Look, Nat, God is using you. Sadly because of your pink situation. But you planted the seed. God will water it." Before Melanie clicked off, she said, "Now go praise Him! He opened the book at Psalm 55:22. It was an affirmation to Gladys that God protects and you will not slip and fall. To you, too."

~

Natalie heard the excitement in Farah's voice. Was that another affirmation?

"God is using you, Natalie." Farah echoed Mel's words.

"But I never asked for that. Why?" she questioned.

Farah laughed so loud Natalie held the phone at arm length. "What's so funny?"

"Surely you know the old adage that God doesn't call the equipped?"

"Yeh, He equips the called. You think He is calling me?"

"Well, He equipped Moses and Aaron, both who argued with Him. Maybe," Farah hesitated, "stop arguing and ask for support. Ask what He wants you to do."

Natalie rubbed her brow and ran her fingers through her hair. How long would she have her hair if she had to have chemo? Was she up to an assignment from God?

~

The call came the next morning. Nat was dressed in sweats ready for work. Time to open the gym. She reluctantly pushed the green button on her phone.

"Need to talk, Natalie." The doctor's voice scared her so she sat down. Maybe she would open the gym a few minutes late. Or Claire would be there on time.

"You are blessed, Ms. Natalie." She was always so impressed he didn't use her surname. Made her feel more comfortable using her given name. But, now? Maybe he was trying to make the conversation, the bad news, more personal.

"Yes, doc?" She gripped her phone tighter.

"I know you went through a lot of physical and emotional trauma with the procedure you had. I know you were scared. I heard about your reaction in the waiting room." He chuckled.

"What, doc? What?" Would the man never get to the point?

"Sorry. We docs tend to drag out information. But this is a fun one. Not fair to you I suppose."

Natalie was sure if she was in his office, face to face, she would have decked him. What was so funny? Not her breast cancer.

Not what doc said about Adam wanting to meet her.

FORTY-SIX

"That's weird," Mel said. "Do docs set up meet and greets between patients and hospital personnel? Oh, my gosh, Nat! You are cancer free! Praise God!"

"Did it suddenly compute?" Nat asked holding her voice in check.

"Guess I was focused on the romance possibility. Of course, I am thrilled! But," she said, "that's what I believed and prayed for all along. Tell me more."

Nat gave a giddy laugh.

"The biopsy was negative. My fears were negative, too. And," she giggled, "I have a date with Adam. Set up by Doctor M. Maybe I will wear my red dress. Glad I saved it."

~

Melanie leaned back on her sofa and opened Draw the Circle by Mark Batterson. The devotions to teach her a new way to pray and change her life in forty days always spoke to her heart. Although reading it for the tenth time, it was always relevant. The other day she took off her sandals like God told Moses to do and stood on

Nat's doorstep to claim the land for Nat's healing. Or was it Joshua He told to do that? Maybe both. She was still learning about prayer and praying. She was learning to be specific in what she asked for in prayer. God wasn't crazy about iffy prayers. Praying wasn't a game to test Him. After all He clearly said "Ask and it will be given to you . . ." He didn't say beg or inquire or question. Although He never said *when* you would get what you asked for, just promised in His time and His will. Was her faith strong enough to get what she asked for and wait for it? Did she believe and not doubt? The Apostle James said if you doubt you could be tossed like the wind. Maybe she should read James 1:6 again. Was that the Scripture? Or was it seven?

She set the Circle book down and stood on the balcony of her condo for some fresh air. Grasping the metal rail helped her steady her thoughts. Sometimes Scripture was confusing, especially if taken out of context. It was windy tonight, and the breeze from the Pacific a few miles away ruffled her hair. Was she doubting? She knew she had pleaded for Natalie, pleaded in faith. Yesterday had been her personally assigned, designated, seventh day to pray for Natalie. Was Nat her Jericho? She had prayed sincerely for the Gladys situation. She chuckled about how Big Bill had turned the woman's grimace into a questioning smile. Nat had been through a lot of fear and anxiety. Although Vivian was right that Nat had no husband to disappoint if she had had breast cancer, she'd also had no man to support her. All the other women did. Noelle, Cindy, Connie, Candy, Doreen, Vivian, even feng shui designer Emily had Nick.

Natalie and I have no one. Maybe now she will if

Adam turns out to be special.

She reached down to pet Lola snuggled at her feet. Lola leaped up and licked her on her nose.

So much for having no one! She laughed and patted the floppy ears.

~

She needed for action to accompany prayer. After all, she was a doer. But sometimes she forgot to do, to combine her prayers with physical actions. She'd prayed circles around Natalie for healing. Not Natalie physically, but often resting her hand over a photo Nat was in or placing her hand on Nat's Gym's business card while praying, and always on the door of Nat's condo. Was it superstition? What about signs and numbers? There were so many examples in the Bible, so many threes and sevens, obviously a thirteen with Jesus and the twelve disciples. Joshua marched around Jericho for seven days, but actually thirteen times in all. God did give signs and symbols. It was very clear, just not to her.

Lola whined and wiggled interrupting Mel's musing. "Need to go out, girl?"

She leashed her and walked Lola around her condo complex breathing in the salty air, wind and all.

The little dog danced on her hind legs and Melanie laughed. "Maybe I should buy you a tutu like Alan suggested."

How long had Alan been in Newport Beach? Surely more than seven days. So much had happened. Must have been way more. Heart pounding, she made a decision, looked at her calendar and dialed his number.

~

"Hi! Ouch!" She heard muffled cursing. "Sorry. Toe stub. Again." He laughed. "Gotta get out of this hotel.

Room too small for me." He took a breath and asked, "You okay? Why are you calling? Hoping to hear from you tonight. Anything wrong?"

Melanie laughed so hard she dropped her phone. Fumbling to retrieve it she laughed again.

"Did you mean what you said the other night? About me, about us? Okay if I put you on Facetime?"

"Just put you on, too. I want to see you. And yes, Melanie, I love you. And I want to spend my life with you."

Melanie held her breath. Did he really mean that? Did he really love her? Could she trust him? She had trusted Larry, then he deceived her. Was she ready to trust again? God had given her a new message this morning in Isaiah 43:19. "For I am about to do something new. See, I have already begun. Do you not see it?" Should she believe that verse was for her? If not, what had prompted her to bring it up on her Bible ap?

She knew in her heart what she desired. Was it time to trust?

"Well," she said in her most deliberately modulated voice. "Lots to tell you, but have a question first."

"Okay, shoot."

Melanie laughed again. Why did men always respond with gun analogies? Maybe she should shoot back.

"So, Alan, how long have you been here in Newport Beach?" She couldn't resist envisioning a fiery arrow whizzing toward his forehead.

When he didn't answer right away, she giggled. "That wasn't a hard question, was it?" Was he pulling up his calendar?

"Seems like ages," he said. "Can you believe it's

only been a week?"

"As in seven days?"

"Guess so. Why?"

Melanie let out a loud whistle. Not exactly the horn the Israelites blew when Jericho's walls tumbled, but it would do.

"Coming over. Unlock the door to room 713."

The End

If you have enjoyed this book please leave a review on Amazon and click on Follow the Author to receive information about my forthcoming books.

Be sure to sign up for my newsletter that morphs into my Facebook author page where I give away books and fun prizes.
http://bonnieengstrom.com/newsletter/
https://www.facebook.com/bonnieengstromauthor/

If you haven't read the entire Candy Cane Series start with Book One, Noelle's Christmas Wedding. Here's a teaser scene from Chapter One.

He'd tried to toss the bouquet off to the side, but there was no time. The Double Delight roses crushed against his forearm sandwiched between his Alpaca sweater and a mane of chestnut hair. His first reaction was to wrap his arms firmly around the limp woman.

The roses finally slipped to the floor with a rustling of Cellophane wrap as he lifted the woman's prone form, not too gracefully, under her shoulders and dragged her onto one of the lobby's overstuffed sofas. Long, thick hair cascaded across her face like a shawl of sepia threads. He heard Jill murmuring behind him and turned to her for advice.

She raised her eyebrows and shrugged. Lacking any guidance he grabbed the recumbent woman's slim ankles and shifted them onto the sofa. Although he felt uncomfortable doing it, he fingered the strands of hair from her face, especially those caught in her open mouth. Reddish-brown eyes that matched the color of her hair flicked open wide. Her beautiful face twisted in fear. At least that was Braydon's first thought.

The Candy Cane Series

Noelle's Christmas Wedding
Cindy's Perfect Dance
Candy's Wild Ride
Connie's Silver Shoes
Natalie's Deception
Melanie's Blue Skirt
Melanie's Ghosts
Doreen Finds Her Groove
Natalie's Red Dress

My Other Books

Butterfly Dreams
A Winning Recipe
When Hearts Entwine
Her Culinary Catch
Restoring Love at Christmastime
A Penney From Heaven
The Matchmaking Wedding Planner
Her Secret Santa

About Bonnie

I've decided I don't like impersonal bios written in the third person. I would rather explain who I am since I know best who I am.

I am a wife, mother, mother-in-law and grandmother who goes by the moniker Grammy. My husband and family are my life. But Jesus is first. He has led me down many paths from PTA volunteer advocating for education for over thirty-five years, newspaper columnist, online prayer chain moderator and author. Each path has been lined with wonderful treasures of love. But the best path has been and still is the Grammy path.

I love the image in Exodus 17:12 of Aaron and Hur lifting up Moses arms. I am blessed to have many Aarons and Hurs holding me up when I get tired. To see six of mine and the one who has held me up for almost 56 years go to my website link below.

Life has taken me from Pittsburgh to Ohio to Washington, D.C. to Los Angeles to Newport Beach and finally to Scottsdale, Arizona living on a lake as I'd dreamed of for years. Yes, Lake Serena is manmade, but

God made the men who made it, and the Canada geese who flock here every winter don't seem to mind. They fly over our house squawking, mess up our street and give us new goslings every Spring. Even our dogs like them.

Dogs are part of my life. Lola, the scruffy one, is on the cover of Melanie's Blue Skirt. Lucy and Sam have cameo appearances in Cindy's Perfect Dance and Melanie's Ghosts respectively. Jake, our precious Min Pin on the cover of Connie's Silver Shoes, is in doggy heaven. Sweet Arthur on the cover of Doreen Finds Her Groove was lent to me for the story by my friend Lisa. Sandy, the Golden Retriever on the cover of A Winning Recipe, is a characterization of Almond Roca, my friend Dorothy's dog who jogged with me for many years. Yes, the Dorothy in the acknowledgements.

Cats have always been important members of our family. Mr. Sunday was first. My mother named him because he came to our door on Sunday. Spats was a rescued laboratory cat when hubby was in grad school. He was super smart and could fetch and play tennis with a ping pong ball. Our kids had Licorice, Mudball who swallowed a needle, Dr. Pepper who insisted on jumping on all laps, Aphrodite who lived to be 21 and a half. Our own children now have Blackey, Vader, Loco, Poco and Bingo.

Now you know who I am. And maybe more about the

stories I write. I hope you like the stories and will read them and post reviews on Amazon and Goodreads. Please check out the links below to contact me. I love to hear from my readers.

www.bonnieengstrom.com (To see the grandchildren and all my books and my writing journey.)

https://www.facebook.com/bonnieengstromauthor/ (Where I give away books and fun stash.)

bengstrom@hotmail.com (Please put BOOKS in the subject line. I love to connect with my readers.)

Milton Keynes UK
Ingram Content Group UK Ltd.
UKHW051341140724
445326UK00014BA/597